FOUR PEBBLES
ON A
BENCH

GARY SLAVIN

PAGE PUBLISHING, INC.
Conneaut Lake, PA

First originally published by Page Publishing 2020

ISBN 978-1-6624-0755-0 (pbk)
ISBN 978-1-6624-0757-4 (hc)
ISBN 978-1-6624-0756-7 (digital)

Printed in the United States of America

CHAPTER 1

It was late June, and the summer humidity in Long Island was already thick in the air. George Price arose at 6:15 a.m., as he did every weekday, to do his morning run at Burns Park while the temperature was still tolerable. It was a large fifty-two-acre park with room for every activity you could imagine: athletic fields for football, soccer, lacrosse, and baseball; courts for handball, basketball, tennis, and boccie ball; paths for walking, running, biking, and rollerblading; playgrounds for the kids; boat ramps; and places to go fishing. As the weather warmed up, more and more people began to show up. On this early Monday morning, George shared the path with groups of women strolling and gossiping, an elderly couple walking, holding hands and laughing as they did their laps, and bike riders pedaling hard to increase their cardio workout.

The whole park was wide open, so you could see what was going on from any spot. Personal trainers were working with their students on one of the turf fields. George, too, was there to train—on his own—trying to stay healthy and keep his heart in tip-top shape. His zeal to stay in shape had started fifteen years earlier, after he had six stents implanted in his arteries to improve blood flow and prevent a heart attack. At the time, he was five foot ten, weighed 230 pounds, and had very high cholesterol. Although he had been an undercover detective with the Nassau County Police Department, he worked in white-collar crime, so he wasn't required to stay fit. His doctor had told him the only thing that would reduce the chance of a heart attack was to lose the extra weight and exercise daily. George took the doctor's advice to heart and got his weight down to 185, where it had stayed for the last decade.

Although he had been retired for five years, his detective instincts were still active, and George never stopped watching people and their actions and took note of the ones who appeared out of the norm. Burns Park had its share of quirky characters—the older white-haired woman who kept a sweater tucked in the back of her sports bra, even in the summer; the Toyota woman who collected empty bottles and cans from the trash bins at the same time every morning (to cash them in for the five-cent refund, George presumed), and the scantily clothed Rollerbladers who seemed to be in their own universe, skating to the beats thumping through their oversize headphones. But mostly everyone was harmless, and George's morning runs were predictable and uneventful. This morning, however, George's detective radar picked up on some unusual activity.

Keeping his pace steady, he watched a tall Italian-looking lady, driving a black Range Rover, stop three quarters around the vehicle pathway, step out, pick up four pebbles, and put them on the left side of the bench in front of the vehicle. Her outfit was typical for a woman working out: tight black running pants with hot pink at the bottom, and her hair was pulled back in a bun, so George assumed she was there for a run. Placing four pebbles on a bench seemed odd, but George thought, *This is New York, and Burns Park attracts a diverse clientele. Things that are out of sort may just fit right in, in the end.*

When George did his next lap, he noticed that one pebble had been moved to the other side of the bench. His initial thought was that it must signify one lap or some time done. When he finished his final lap, all four pebbles had been moved to the other side of the bench, and the car was gone. But George thought it was very strange that he hadn't seen the woman running on the path. He would have passed her or at least should have seen her across the way at some point. But he was in a rush that day, so he didn't give it too much more thought.

The next few days were back to the usual routine and usual crowd: everyone came for their flavor of activity then left. But on Friday, the black Range Rover was back. The same woman—again dressed for a workout, except this time her outfit was all black, and this time she seemed to be in a rush, and she wasn't as put together as she had been—quickly got out of the car, picked up four pebbles, and walked away from the vehicle. Now George's retired-detective instincts were really piqued, especially since a glass bottle of beer fell out of her car as she opened the door. *Who is this lady?* George thought. Out of the corner of his eye, George noticed a police car with lights flashing rounding the corner and coming to a complete stop behind the Range Rover, blocking the car. The officers quickly left their car. One went to investigate the car, while the other ran after the lady. As the officer caught up to the lady, George overheard him giving her, her Miranda rights. George turned to the officer investigating the car and asked, "What is she being arrested for?"

"Oh, hey, George," the officer replied. "DUI. She is on something, she hit a bicyclist and left the scene about a half-mile down on Merrick Road."

"Is the bicyclist okay?" George asked.

"No," the officer replied in a very aggravated tone and then showed George the blood on his pants. George couldn't believe how much blood was on the officer's pants.

George spent the weekend thinking of possible scenarios to explain the strange activity and arrived on Monday hoping to find a few more clues. Unfortunately, there was no suspicious activity that morning; so again, George put it out of his mind.

That Wednesday was the Fourth of July. After returning from another uneventful run at the park, George turned on the local news channel, FiOS1, to determine whether he felt like dealing with the traffic to get to the annual holiday barbecue at his in-laws'. But instead of a traffic report, the top story was about how Nassau County officials were reminding people to stay vigilant this Fourth of July holiday after a recent spike of drug overdoses in the Massapequa area. Officials said that in the past thirteen days, six overdoses had been linked to a potentially lethal batch of heroin. Four of the overdose victims died from the lethal heroin—one woman and three men, including a twenty-four-year-old man whose overdose resulted in the apprehension of one suspect.

"Within three hours, the Nassau County Police Department arrested the drug dealer who was involved in that death," stated Chief of Detectives Tom Daily. Early Sunday morning, police had arrested twenty-one-year-old Edward Gillespie of Corona in Massapequa Park. Police said he had unlawfully possessed and sold a tan powdery substance in wax paper envelopes, believed to be heroin, to someone in that area. Chief of Detectives Daily stated, "We have already had six overdoses in Massapequa. I'm asking every parent to know where your children are and what they are doing this long holiday weekend. I don't want to attend any more overdose funerals." Daily concluded the press briefing with, "Gillespie will be charged with criminal possession and sale of a controlled substance."

George decided to gamble with the traffic and ended up staying at the family barbecue until after midnight, giving him enough time to wait out the after-fireworks crowd and make it home without too much trouble. Since he had made good food choices at the barbecue and stayed out later than usual, he gave himself the day off from running on Thursday.

But on Friday, he was back to his routine. This week, no Range Rover showed up, but a dark-blue Ferrari California T did. Since George did a lot of his undercover work with car insurance agencies, he knew that this car cost around $235,000—not your typical run-to-the-park activity car. Another Italian-looking woman got out of the vehicle. She was wearing the same type of outfit as the Range Rover lady, only her outfit was white with silver trim on her pants, and her brown hair was down, almost covering her face. As George ran by, again keeping his pace steady so that it wasn't obvious he was watching, he noticed her bending down to pick up four pebbles. She placed them on the left side of the bench, just as the Range Rover lady had done. George didn't get to see where she went because he passed her and didn't want to draw attention by looking back her way. But the scene played out exactly the same: each lap George did, another pebble was moved to the other side, and by his fourth lap, the Ferrari had disappeared.

As George finished his laps, he thought, *Twice is a coincidence. But three times, with the pebbles on the bench, something is going on.*

As he got home, his cell phone rang. It was his good friend Neil Vincent. Neil was six foot two and was also a veteran undercover detective, but he had worked in the drug unit. He had been involved with every major undercover investigation in Nassau County and had finished up his career as the bodyguard to the county executive. At fifty-nine, he still looked like a pro-football lineman.

"Hi, Neil, what's up?" George asked.

"George, I need to catch up with you. How is Sunday at noon?" Neil replied.

"Okay, but I can't do it until after mass. How about one thirty?"

"Sure, that works," said Neil.

"At the Nautilus Diner?" George asked.

"Of course! Where else would we meet?" said Neil.

"Okay, see you then."

After mass, George drove to the Nautilus, a Greek diner in business for over sixty years and a staple in the Massapequa community for business meetings, charity fundraisers, takeouts, or chatting with old friends. By the time George got to the diner, Neil had already taken a booth and ordered them both coffee and a bagel.

"Neil, before you start, I have to tell you what's going on at Burns," George said urgently. George and Neil had known each other since their first days in the Nassau County Police Academy. In their early career days, before they both received promotions to different units, they worked on many cases together and protected each other's backs. George knew he could trust Neil and count on him for anything, and he was eager to get his take on what was going on at Burns Park.

"What do you mean?" Neil asked.

"Black Range Rovers and blue Ferraris," George stated.

"What, are you looking for a new car?" Neil said with a laugh.

George replied, "No. Let me start from the beginning. As you know, I've been running laps at Burns. Two weeks ago, a black Range Rover turned into the park. It drove past the football field and past the boat ramp parking lot and parked in one of the diagonal parking spaces across from the challenger baseball field, south of the soccer field. I noticed an Italian woman getting out of the car and walking slowly to the front. She picked up four pebbles and placed them on one side of the bench, close together. Then she started to walk north toward the front of the park. She had on a black-and-pink outfit, and she looked athletic. I never saw her again, but on each lap I did passing the car, one of the pebbles had been moved to the other side. At first I thought she was using the rocks to keep track of her laps, but I never saw her again. The car had left by my fourth lap, and all the pebbles were on the other side of the bench. At first I thought it was strange, but whatever."

"When was this?"

"Monday, June 25. Then again on Friday, June 29, same woman comes, and she parks in the same spot and then gets arrested for DUI and hit-and-run," said George.

"Interesting," Neil said.

"But on Friday the sixth, a blue Ferrari shows up, and this time another Italian lady gets out of the car and does the same thing—picks up four pebbles and places them on the same bench as the Range Rover lady did."

"Is this parking spot near the high grass, dense brush, or trees near the preserve?" asked Neil.

"Yes, why?"

"Once a cop, always a cop. I think you found a drug ring," said Neil. "When I worked for the town of Oyster Bay in the public safety marine unit, our boats were parked there overnight. The guys in the park used to hear stuff at night from the high grass, but they thought it was an animal looking for food, so they never looked into it. One morning, after hearing a lot of noise at night, I decided to find out what type of animal was making all this noise."

"Yeah, so what did you see?" George asked.

"Nothing," said Neil. "My partner wanted to leave and get to the bay and safeguard the community."

"Yeah, right," George replied.

"But seriously, George. You know three isn't a coincidence. What are you going to do?" asked Neil.

"I want to see what happens tomorrow. If the Range Rover or the blue Ferrari or a third car shows up and a lady picks up four pebbles and places them on the bench, we got a problem," stated George.

On Monday, George woke up early, anticipating who and what was going to show. He left his house at the usual time so as not to screw up the schedule. When George got to Burns Park, there seemed to be too many unfamiliar faces. When he started his laps, he realized that all the new faces were probably undercover cops. The two couples jogging were a little too fit; by their looks, their workout would be more demanding than a light jog around the park. The three others had the wrong outfits for outside exercise. One had a bulge in his sock—probably his backup revolver. Once he saw that, George knew Neil must have called NCPD and alerted them to their conversation. George wondered why Neil would have done that and thought, *He really blew this.*

At first, he wanted to call Neil and ask him why the hell he did that. But then he started to wonder, *Did Neil's phone call somehow warn the Range Rover or Ferrari ladies? Or was there someone in the park who saw the unfamiliar faces and alerted them?*

As George was running, he caught his foot on an exposed water sprinkler pipe and fell to the ground. Immediately, he put out his hands to brace his fall. As his body hit the ground, he saw six portable bathrooms behind the bleachers and tall evergreens that he had never noticed before. He quickly got up to check for broken bones or cuts. Thank God, there was none.

George wondered how he had missed this hidden space with six port-a-potties. As he walked back to his car, he tried to piece together the footsteps of the Range Rover and Ferrari ladies. Did they go there? Could the four pebbles have something to do with the port-a-potties? Without proof or further evidence, he could only speculate.

On Tuesday, George decided he should start watching anyone who walked near the hidden toilets. One of the visitors that day was the tall white-haired woman who always jogged with a sweater hanging on the back of her neck. She wore a white baseball cap, with The End inscribed in red on the back. George watched her more closely today and saw that she drove a white Volkswagen Passat, which she had parked three spaces down from the bench where the pebbles were placed. She walked across the soccer field, opened the gate

CHAPTER 2

George arose Wednesday morning eager to get to the park to continue observing the people and any suspicious activity. As he drove around the park to the front parking lot, he noticed a woman doing ballet exercises next to a white 4 × 4 Jeep Wrangler. George quickly parked and began his jog around the park, anxious to get to the bench near the Jeep. As he came around the corner, he was surprised to see five pebbles on the bench, with one pebble already moved to the other side. The ballet woman had already disappeared by the time George reached the bench; he couldn't see her anywhere in the park. He thought it would be too conspicuous if he went to the port-a-potties, so he stuck with his original routine. He decided to jog faster in the hopes of finding this mysterious woman, but he never saw her. When he got to the bench again, another pebble had been moved. Three more laps and all the remaining pebbles had been moved, and the white Jeep was gone.

Thursday was a quiet morning at the park until George's last lap. After three laps on the jogging path, he decided to jog around the entire park's perimeter. This route took him down to the canal surrounding the park, the boat docks and boat launch, the town maintenance building, then back up to the athletic fields, where the port-a-potties were. On his last lap, he saw a white Sea Ray boat coming slowly up the canal. The lady at the controls was about forty, wearing a white floral-embroidered beach cover-up, but the slight breeze blew the cover-up back enough to show her white two-piece bathing suit. When she got close enough to the dock, she quickly secured the rope and made a beeline run toward the port-a-potties. She ran through the parking lot, scaring the Canada geese out of her way, cutting her way between the two little league baseball diamonds across the large natural-grass practice field. Finally reaching the back of the soccer field, she took a white pouch out of her pocket and dropped it into the green steel garbage can and went into the fourth port-a-potty. It seemed like only seconds later when the lady in white sprinted out of the port-a-potties back to the boat. Off she went, leaving no wake and hopefully no suspicions of the criminal activity that just occurred. George laughed when he saw the name on the boat, No Names.

Just as George was about to head back to the main path to get back to his car, he noticed a gray Toyota Camry pull up near the port-a-potties. The Toyota woman was there to collect her daily ration of bottles and cans. As usual, she had brought several large trash bags, which she was able to fill since Burns was such a big active park. When she looked in the trash can that the white pouch had been dropped in, her body became stiff, unable to move because her mind was processing what to do. She quickly put the pouch in her pocket and jogged to her car, dragging the nearly full plastic trash bag behind her. She tossed the trash bag in the back seat, got in, and sped off.

The Sea Ray meandered slowly back down the canal, passing the homes of the rich and the almost famous. As she got closer to her destination, a man started yelling to her from the dock.

"Caroline! Caroline, where have you been?" asked Jonathan.

"Shhh, Jonathan, you'll wake the neighbors," replied Caroline in a loud whisper.

"Are you for real? You leave the house at six thirty in the morning to take the boat for a ride? Where have you been?" Jonathan demanded.

Caroline docked the boat and said, "Come on, let's go inside the house. Our neighbors don't need to hear you!"

Jonathan Mack was a fifty-year-old retired group-insurance executive; he had made his money before Obamacare. Once Obamacare was passed, he did presentations to his large clients and national business groups about the future effects of Obamacare on the health-care business. At that time, they didn't believe him. Four short years later, his predictions were dead-on. He had predicted that premiums would be unaffordable, especially for families, because the new law only mandated that an employee's contribution be capped at 9.86 percent of the employee's salary, but employers were not required to provide the same cap for the employee's family members. When Obamacare ran into trouble, the Obama White House called him for solutions. His recommendation was to repeal the entire law except for the provision that eliminated the preexisting-conditions clause in medical policies and repeal the employee contributions cap and go back to a system where employers gave their employees money to spend on the health care that worked for them. He even sent the White House a draft of the bill that could be passed in all fifty states and federally. The White House's response was "no comment."

Jonathan was in good shape; after he retired, he started training to climb mountains. His goal was to climb mountains on every continent. He knew the allure of drugs because at the beginning of his career, he worked in Downtown Manhattan, where he did a lot of late-night business deals in bars. Drugs were plentiful there, and he started using cocaine and then switched to Adderall because it was easier to get. All this was so he could continue working eighteen- to twenty-hour days. It wasn't until he totaled his car after one of those late-night deals that he realized his days were numbered if he continued down that path. The cop who pulled him out of the car before it burst into flames gave him an Alcoholics Anonymous card. With the help of AA, he got his life back on track and eventually became a born-again Christian.

Caroline was his longtime girlfriend. He would have married her several times, but she had a drug habit. Jonathan had met her at work. She was a natural blonde beauty, intelligent, and able to have a heart-to-heart conversation with anyone without being offensive, and some of Jonathan's clients needed that. And she knew the health-care business. Her first husband had died of a painkiller overdose. Jonathan always thought her addiction was because Caroline blamed herself for his overdose, since she was in their home when he took the final dose.

They walked into Jonathan's home, and Caroline closed the sliding glass door behind her to protect her neighbors from what could turn into a loud argument. Jonathan repeated his questions.

"Where did you go?"

"For a drive. I needed space and quiet," Caroline replied.

"Bullshit. You went to the Burns Park again, didn't you?" Jonathan yelled out.

"I drove up that way, but no, I didn't stop at Burns. I was looking at all the rich and the to-be-famous owners' backyards. You know, Jonathan, you have the best backyard," Caroline replied.

"We have the best backyard, but don't change the subject," Jonathan replied at a more normal conversational level. "But for me to believe you," Jonathan continued, "I need to check your pockets."

"What? No!" Caroline yelled back.

"Caroline," Jonathan spoke in a calm, strong, controlling voice, "we have a deal, remember? We...*I*...can't have any drugs in this house, and you know why. I need to check your pockets."

"I don't like it, but I did agree to it. And yes, I understand why," Caroline responded. Caroline knew once she had heard Jonathan's voice on the dock that this was coming, so she had hidden the drugs on the boat. "Okay, do you want to search my pockets now or after I clean the boat?" Caroline asked.

"Now!" Jonathan replied in a firm voice.

Jonathan started to search Caroline's pockets, but his fingers quickly moved to other parts of her body.

"I don't have pockets in those areas," Caroline proclaimed.

"I know. Just trying to be thorough," Jonathan replied with a smile, his tone finally softening, relieved that her pockets were empty.

"Why don't we move to the bedroom then, so you can do a full-body search?" Caroline was smiling now too. They slowly made their way to the bedroom, laughing and kissing on the way.

Thursday night was a long night for George. His mind was spinning, trying to put together all the pieces of the puzzle—the port-a-potties, the boat lady, the Toyota woman, and the sweater lady. He couldn't discuss this with his wife; she would just blow up at him for getting involved. And if he told Neil, George was afraid he would call the NCPD and everything would come to a halt. So he decided to say nothing and just watch and take mental notes.

On Friday, George went back to his port-a-potty observations. As he was jogging by the great lawn used for concerts under the stars, the sweater lady had just pulled up in her Volkswagen. She got out of the car, walked across the soccer field, and headed toward the port-a-potties area, just as she had done last time. As George rounded the bend, she was already on her way back to the soccer field, but she was walking very quickly and seemed to be upset and afraid. Instead of going to the jogging path, she immediately got in her Passat and drove away. *No workout for her today*, George thought.

As George was pondering what could have happened at the port-a-potties to elicit such an emotional reaction, his attention was turned to the sound of a large pickup truck pulling up. It was the town crew, there to make their daily rounds of cleaning out the trash cans in the park. That was when George realized that the Toyota lady hadn't shown up to collect her cans. She always got there fifteen minutes earlier than the town crew, which always angered the one with a handlebar mustache. He was also trying to collect any empties to cash in on the five-cent refund. When he saw the trash can full of empty soda bottles, his eyes widened. With a huge grin, he ran back to the truck to get a plastic garbage bag. With Toyota lady gone, Mr. Handlebar Mustache got the loot.

That night, George couldn't believe what he saw on the news. At eleven o'clock, News 12 reported that a white woman with white hair was found dead in a white Volkswagen Passat parked on a dead-end street in Brightwaters, near the Great South Bay. The woman had no ID, and the police suspected it was another drug overdose. But to be sure, they needed to run a toxicology exam, said the reporter.

George switched over to FiOS1, which showed an interview with the neighbor who had called 911.

The reporter started the interview with, "The neighbor has requested we interview him off camera. Okay, sir, describe in your own words what happened tonight."

"My wife and I had just gotten back from a party around nine o'clock, and I wanted to take the dog for a walk before I went to bed.

As we walked down the block, I saw a car with no lights on parked. I immediately thought it was kids having fun in the car, but I noticed there wasn't any movement in the car. As I got closer, I noticed all the windows were rolled up, which I thought was odd because it is a warm night. When I saw the driver slumped over the passenger seat, I knocked on the window to see if she was all right. When she didn't move, I opened the door and kind of poked her and said, 'Hey, wake up.' I got no reaction, so that was when I dialed 911."

"What type of car was it?" asked the reporter.

"Volkswagen," replied the witness.

The reporter asked, "Have you given your statement to the police?"

"Yes, but I have to finish walking my dog. Bye."

The reporter turned and looked into the camera and said, "There you have the whole story from the individual who found the woman in the car. Stay tuned to FiOS1 for more updates on this story."

As George listened to the news, he already knew this wasn't an overdose. The Volkswagen woman was probably killed because she was careless with the drug ring's money, and a message had to be sent.

CHAPTER 3

On Saturday morning, George was eager to call Neil and fill him in on his latest park observations and how they tied in with the death of Volkswagen or sweater woman. He made the call from his home office to make sure his wife didn't overhear. Being married to a detective had been a challenge for her, but their marriage had survived. He didn't want her to know that he was getting involved with another case in his retirement.

"Hey, Neil, it's George."

"Good morning, George. How are you doing?"

"Good. Did you hear about that woman in Brightwaters who was found dead in her car?" asked George.

"Yeah, I watched it last night on FiOS1. Why?" asked Neil.

"That's the Volkswagen woman at Burns!"

"Is that the sweater woman you were telling me about a couple days ago?"

"Yep. Listen, Neil, do not call your friends at the department."

"They're your friends too," said Neil.

"Yeah right, but we need to meet at Burns first. I think there are bigger things going on than the sweater woman," George said.

"Okay, when?" Neil asked.

"Monday at six thirty a.m."

"Why so early?" Neil asked.

"Because that's when the cast of characters shows up," George told him. "And promise me you are not going to call the department until after we discuss this and we agree it's time to bring them in."

"Why?" Neil asked. "You're retired. I'm retired. Why not let the rookies in the department handle it?"

"For a couple reasons, Neil. One, it's our community. And two, my gut is telling me that this is a very sophisticated criminal organization with the ability to stay below the radar. We, or I, need to sort this all out before bringing in the department because they are likely to only go after the murder of sweater woman and forget about the rest. You know even better than I do that Massapequa has a drug problem and has had one for the past twenty years, and—"

"Okay, okay," Neil interrupted, "you made your point. You're right, and I'm on board. But we're going to need a CI—a confidential informant."

"Neil, remember," George replied, "I did white-collar crime. You did the undercover drug and prostitution busts. Do you still know any CIs?"

Neil replied, "Let's meet on Tuesday instead of Monday so I have time to come up with some people I know who might help us. Oh, Burns is over fifty-two acres. Where exactly are we going to meet?"

"By the port-a-potties behind the bleachers by the soccer field. It's in between the baseball field and the soccer field, okay?"

"Okay, see you then. Goodbye, George." George hung up the phone and sat in his office, thinking. This would be a good test to see if Neil could really keep this between just them. If he blabbered this to the department, it would be over. The criminal ring would scatter, never to be found again. But George felt he had no choice. Neil had the contacts in the drug and prostitution rings. George could only read a financial report and tell whether or not someone was embezzling money from the company. *I guess I'll find out Tuesday morning if I can trust Neil and if he still has his contacts,* George thought.

"George," his wife called from upstairs.

"Yes, honey?"

"Did you have breakfast?" she asked.

"No."

"Do you want me to fix you something to eat?"

"No, but I'll have coffee with you," he replied.

"Who were you talking to?" she asked.

"A client," he replied. When George retired, he became an expert witness for insurance companies on employee dishonesty claims. If George had told her that it was Neil, there would have been another fifty questions. You'd think she was a retired detective instead of a retired art teacher.

George was a little relieved that Monday was uneventful at the park. No fancy cars, no ballet dancers, no pebbles. It gave him another day to mull over the sequence of events and plan for his meeting with Neil.

Tuesday morning finally came, and Neil showed up on time, carrying a file in hand. George asked, "What's with the file?"

"I'll go through it with you later. First, walk me through what you saw," said Neil.

"Okay. Thursday morning, I started my usual jog around the bend. By the beginning of the great lawn, I saw a white Sea Ray boat come up the canal. The female driver docked the boat by the boat launch, sprinted across the parking lot through the baseball fields to this trash can where she dropped a white pouch, then proceeded directly to port-a-potty number 4. She stayed there for what seemed seconds and proceeded to sprint back to the boat, leaving with no wake. The name on the boat was No Names.

"Shortly afterward, the Toyota woman came to the trash can. She started her usual picking, then I could see her body stiffen. She pulled out the white pouch and put it into her pants pocket. Then she ran as fast as she could, dragging the trash bag of empty cans and bottles to her car. She drove off quickly and then wasn't back Friday morning. And we know what happened Friday night."

"Okay, what do you think happened?" Neil asked.

"I think the white pouch that Sea Ray lady dropped in the trash had money in it to pay for the drugs that she retrieved from the port-a-potty. Then early Friday morning, a tall white-haired lady, about seventy—"

"Is this the sweater woman?" Neil interrupted.

"Yes," George replied. "She also wears a baseball cap with The End in red printed on the back. She did her usual routine, parked her car near the bench with the pebbles and walked across the soccer field to the port-a-potties. But this time, after looking in the trash can, she quickly walked backed to her car and sped away. I saw her face. She looked angry and afraid. I guess she was mad at whoever stole her money, which we know was the Toyota woman."

"George, if you know that, the drug ring will realize it soon too," Neil said. Neil explained to George how a drug organization was structured. The sweater woman was called a runner, who'd get the drugs to the addict or user. She was controlled by the first-line manager, or pusher, who had managers above him. All these lines of management were in place to do one thing: protect Mr. or Ms. Big so their hands never touch the stuff.

"You mean plausible deniability?" George asked.

"Yep, you got it," Neil replied. "But the woman in real trouble is the Toyota woman. She has, or had, the drug ring's money, and you haven't seen her?"

"Nope," George replied.

Neil continued, "I imagine the pusher is trying to find her. Oh God, more trouble." With all of Neil's experience, he could write the story that would be in tomorrow's paper about what was going to happen to Toyota woman. "Okay, there really is only one outcome," Neil concluded.

"You think they're going to kill her?" George asked. "Like what they did to the sweater woman?"

"No. Toyota woman is a civilian. Killing her would bring too much heat, too many cops investigating her death, maybe even family. Losing one drop bag was a serious problem for the runner because she was careless with their money. But Toyota lady doesn't know where the money came from, so it's not as serious of an offense. Let's say the pouch had $250 in it—not enough money to risk the potential attention her death could bring. They want the money back, for sure, and they don't want this to happen again. So they are probably going to find Toyota woman and rough her up to teach her a lesson and make sure she never takes their money again."

"Rough her up?" George asked, sounding concerned.

"Toyota woman will be alive but, in the end, will have several broken bones and a lot of painful contusions. That will send the message 'Don't fuck with our money.'"

CHAPTER 4

Annie Smith (sweater woman) had been a hardworking woman her whole life. She was a product of the school of hard knocks, and she spent her entire childhood getting shuffled around the foster-care system. With no family to help out, she was constantly looking for odd jobs, sometimes working two or three at a time just to make ends meet. Being a runner for the drug ring meant she finally had enough money to take care of herself and quit all her other jobs—but the downside was, if she screwed up, there could be harsh consequences. Sitting in her car on the dead-end street, waiting for the inevitable visit from Davie, her pusher, she clenched her white sweater as she reviewed the events in her life that led her down this path. She was not looking forward to the conversation and was terrified of the consequences.

The sudden click of the passenger door opening startled her back to reality. "Hey, Annie, where's the money?"

"Davie, there was a minor problem, but I know who has it," said Annie with a shaky voice. As the first-line manager, in corporate speak, Davie was not someone you wanted to displease. She knew she was in trouble but tried to downplay her mistake and appease him by offering to fix it.

"Listen, I know I screwed up, but I can get the money back."

"Okay, Annie," Davie said in a calm but patronizing tone, "what happened?"

"Caroline called me, and she said she needed an emergency fix. So instead of following the usual procedure, I told her to leave the money in the trash bins by the potties."

"Caroline didn't pay you?" Davie blurted out, his voice now showing how pissed he was.

"No, no, she paid." Annie was getting more nervous and scared as she spoke. Finally, she shouted out, "It was the bottle lady!"

Davie's face squinted in confusion. "The *bottle* lady? The one who drives the Toyota? She has my money?" asked Davie, still not quite sure she was telling the truth.

"Yes," answered Annie, "but don't worry, I can get it back."

"How do you know it's the bottle lady who's got my money?" asked Davie.

"Because every morning, she goes through each trash bin to get the bottles for the five-cent refund," replied Annie. "I see her there every morning."

"So let me get this straight. You told Caroline to drop my money in a trash bin that you know will be checked out by this bottle lady. Do I even want to know why you weren't at the trash bin immediately after Caroline dropped my money in there?"

"Because you always told me to wait. It looks suspicious if I walk right up to the bin after a drop was made," explained Annie, clearly trying to save her life.

"How are you going to get it back?" Davie asked, again with a note of sarcasm and disbelief. His body language was showing he was getting angrier by the moment.

"She lives in her car at the Massapequa mall, behind the closed Toys R Us building," Annie said, hoping the added information would give her a new lease on life.

"That's not going to be your concern. I'll handle bottle lady, and *you* are going to take a long sleep." With no time for Annie to react, Davie grabbed her arm, stuck a needle in it, and watched her die. To make sure the cops thought it was an accidental overdose, Davie took Annie's lifeless hand and placed her fingers on the syringe.

As he got out of the white Passat, a black Escalade pulled up. Out stepped a muscular six-foot-tall man with big hands and wavy hair. He was Davie's boss, Warren Santaniello.

"Did you get the information?" Warren asked.

"Yep," Davie answered. "We need to go to the Holiday Plaza Mall in Massapequa by the old Toys R Us. That's where our money is."

Davie jumped into Warren's vehicle, and they immediately headed to the mall. "This better happen" was all Warren said to Davie on the way. As much as Annie had feared Davie's wrath, Davie feared crossing Warren even more. But he was sure that getting their money back from a homeless, can-collecting woman would be an easy day.

"Don't worry. I have it under control," replied Davie cockily.

The Holiday Plaza Mall sat on a large rectangular property, with the entrance and exit on the front short end facing Sunrise Highway. On the other three sides, the owner had installed an eight-foot fence to mark the property line. Along the longer sides of the rectangle were the major department stores and all freestanding buildings, including the Toys R Us that was in the rear section of the large parking lot directly behind the building was the fence. And on the other side of the fence was a high school football field with stands that blocked the view of the back of the building. Between the building and the field was a small stream, which was fed by an underground river that eventually led into the Carmans River. When they arrived at the defunct toy store, they saw a Toyota parked behind the building, just like Annie had said. The bottle lady had backed her car into the spot behind the building because if there was ever a problem, she could drive right out for a quick getaway. Warren parked his Escalade front to front with the Toyota, almost anticipating the bottle lady's next move.

"Okay, Davie, get my money," Warren instructed.

As Davie walked to the passenger side of Maryann's car, she thought she should have used some of the money she found to fix the car door locks, which hadn't worked in a while. But thinking about that now wasn't going to help her immediate situation.

Davie opened the passenger-side door and got in.

"Lady, you got my money. Hand it over," Davie demanded in a menacing tone. He was hoping to get the money quickly and get home.

"I don't know you, and I sure as hell don't have any money," the bottle lady responded.

"Let me make this perfectly clear. You took money out of a green garbage bin on Thursday at Burns Park. That is my money. Where is it?" Davie asked.

"Oh, that money? I don't have it. It's gone."

"That's too bad," said Davie.

"Too bad for whom?" the bottle lady asked, not showing any sign of fear but wishing the angry thug would get out of her car.

"For you," Davie replied.

"I don't think so!" Almost immediately, her military training came back to her; and with one twist of his neck, Davie was gone.

Warren had watched the entire scene from the front seat of the Escalade. He was impressed with the way she had handled herself and immediately thought about how he could use her. Warren signaled to her with two blinks of his headlights, hoping she understood that he came in peace. She responded with two flashes from her car. Warren got out and strolled toward her driver's side window.

"Hey, lady, we need to talk," Warren said. "Let's meet at the Nautilus Diner in twenty minutes. Do you know where it is?"

"Yeah, but what am I to do with your buddy?" she asked.

"Push Davie out and drive to the diner. I'll take care of him."

As the Toyota lady pulled out from behind the vacant building, she pushed Davie's body out of her car and onto the ground. She hadn't felt a dead, lifeless body since the war. As his body hit the ground, her first thought was, *I hope I'm not the next dead body on the ground.* But then her survival instincts snapped back in, and she thought, *Hell no. Not me. I will survive!*

Warren was on his cell phone. "Hey, Mark, I have a job for you. Davie screwed up again. He's behind the old Toys R Us building at the mall. Can you take care of this?"

"Sure. Vacuum and clean?" Mark replied.

"Yes, exactly. Thanks, Mark. Good night," answered Warren.

As Warren pulled into the Nautilus parking lot, he saw the Toyota parked, with the bottle woman still inside. He walked by the car and waved to her to follow him in. As Warren walked by her, she watched him and thought he looked familiar. Then it came to her: a scruffy Indiana Jones. By his walk, she could tell that he was a man who gets what he wants.

Once inside the diner, Warren walked straight back to the conference area and got the last table, next to the emergency door and in full view of the windows and the parking lot. He saw the Toyota lady get out of her car and start walking toward the diner's front door. Just then, Evan, Warren's favorite waiter, came over to the table.

"Good evening, Warren," said Evan.

"Hey, Evan, can you get me two cups of coffee and two medium-rare cheeseburgers with fries on one and the other just the hamburger?" asked Warren.

"Yes, right away," said Evan.

"Okay, thanks," said Warren. As Evan left, the Toyota lady sat down.

"So what do you want to talk about?" she barked out.

"Calm down. I ordered you a coffee and a hamburger with fries. Relax," Warren spoke calmly and gave a small smile. "First, what's your name?"

"Why?" demanded Toyota lady.

"I'm writing a book, and I don't want to keep calling you bottle lady, okay?" Warren stated sarcastically.

Toyota lady gave a heavy sigh and then acquiesced. "Maryann Murphy," she replied, sounding slightly defeated.

"Good. Maryann, I saw what you did tonight. You have military training, don't you?" Warren asked.

"Yes. Two tours in Afghanistan. Special Forces," replied Maryann.

Warren looked at her skeptically. "Women weren't able to join Special Forces until 2016. You couldn't have done two tours. Don't lie to me, bottle lady."

Maryann smiled and replied, "You know your history. Women have been allowed to serve on the front lines and undercover in the CIA since World War II. My technical title was liaison to the DOD."

Before Warren could reply, Evan came to the table with the hamburgers. "Who gets the one with the fries?" Warren pointed to Maryann, whose eyes grew wide as Evan set down the burger with a huge stack of french fries on the side. "Is there anything else I can get you?" Evan asked.

"Not now. Maybe later," Warren replied.

"*Mangia, mangia*," Warren told Maryann. "We'll talk after you finish your hamburger."

Maryann finished her burger and began to eat the fries when Warren started to explain her situation and what he wanted from her.

"Maryann, I know you can't pay me back for the money that you took, so I'm going to need you to work it off."

Maryann's eyes went wide, and she started shaking her head and said, "No way. No way!"

"Don't worry," Warren said, a little offended at her reaction, "I'm not asking for sex! But since Davie is gone, I need someone to take his place. You will be paid. Enough to find an apartment to live in instead of living in your car."

"What did Davie do?" Maryann asked.

"He was my runner," replied Warren.

"*Drug* runner?" Maryann asked, looking around to see if anyone was listening.

Warren nodded his head as he took a big sip of his coffee and stared at Maryann, carefully watching her every movement and facial expression. As he nodded, Maryann's eyes hit the floor. Her body language was telling Warren that she was struggling with the job offer. The quiet at the table reminded Maryann of a fight she was in, in Afghanistan, so much so that her left leg where she had been wounded began to twitch. She began to sink low in her chair, as if to avoid incoming bullets or bombs. Just then, Evan walked to the table. "Hi again. Is everyone done?"

Warren nodded and motioned for Evan to take Maryann's plate.

"Does anyone want dessert?" Evan asked.

Maryann slowly slid back up into her chair. The flashback was over, and she returned to the present time in the Nautilus.

"What's your favorite dessert?" Warren asked Evan.

"I have three favorites: the carrot cake, the cheesecake with the blueberries, and my all-time favorite, tiramisu," Evan said with a smile, as if he could taste the tiramisu.

Warren said, "I'll have your all-time favorite, the tiramisu."

Evan said, "Great choice, Warren." He turned to Maryann and asked, "Miss, would you like any dessert?"

"Cheesecake without blueberries and more coffee," Maryann replied.

As Evan walked away, Maryann looked straight into Warren's face and said, "I don't know if I can do it." She remembered those words coming out of her mouth once before, just after she got her first mission briefing from her commanding officer. He had smiled, put his hand on her shoulder, and said, "Soldier, we are all a little weak in the knees the first time out. You will do just fine. Just remember your training, and everything will click when the fighting starts."

Warren was far from being as polite and reassuring as her former commanding officer was. His response was simple and direct. "Look, Maryann, you have two choices: do the job or end up like Davie. It is your choice but my timetable. Do you understand me?" Warren raised his voice a little to make his point. At that moment, Evan came to the table with dessert.

"Okay, Warren, you get the tiramisu. And, miss, you get the cheesecake without blueberries. More coffee is on the way."

Maryann looked up at Evan and smiled to thank him for his service.

As soon as Evan walked away and was out of earshot, Warren leaned across the table and asked, "Do we have a deal?"

"I guess I don't have much choice," Maryann replied.

"No, you don't," Warren said firmly. Just then, his cell phone beeped. It was a text message from Mark: "All cleaned up. Good night." Warren put the phone facedown on the table and took another phone from his pocket. Maryann immediately knew it was a burner phone, like the ones she had confiscated from the Taliban.

"This is your business phone," Warren explained. "You will be getting calls and text messages from your customers, telling you which items they need. Your job is to deliver the goods and pick up the money. When you're not using the phone, take the battery out. Always have the battery in and phone on between five thirty a.m.

and seven thirty a.m. and again from six thirty p.m. to nine thirty p.m. It's almost eight thirty now. Take the phone and go back to the Toys R Us building. Write down in detail every message you get, voice mail or text, and we will meet tomorrow at four in the morning at the Massapequa Diner. Remember, take the battery out of the phone when you're done. Welcome to the retail business."

"Yeah, the *illegal* retail business," Maryann replied.

Warren laughed and said, "For now. Tomorrow, it could be legal." He got up from the table and motioned to Evan for the bill. He paid the bill and left Maryann to finish her cheesecake alone.

On the way home, Warren couldn't stop thinking about Maryann. He could see that underneath the scraggly long black hair, baggy clothes, and disheveled look, she was an attractive woman. But it was more than that—and not just her impressive military instincts. There was something else that drew him to her, but he couldn't quite figure out what it was. He had to set those feelings aside though. He was still the boss, and he had a reputation to live up to.

Maryann sat in the chair and played with her cheesecake as she wondered how she got to this point. *I fought for this country, obeyed all the rules. Now I'm selling drugs to stay alive! Where's the fucking silver lining?*

"Hi, miss, would you like any more coffee?" Evan asked.

"No, but do you know this guy Warren?" Maryann asked him.

"He's a regular. Seems like a nice guy, and tips well," Evan said.

"Do you know what he does for a living?" Maryann wanted to find out as much as possible about her new boss.

"I think he's an insurance broker or does investments. Something like that," Evan answered. "Well, have a good night, miss. Hope to see you again."

Maryann drove back to the Toys R Us building, not sure if she should stay another night or try to find another spot. As she looked at the tall one-story building, she thought about how long it had taken her to find a place like this. It was close to the areas she needed to go to get the bottles. The parking spot behind the building was secluded from view, yet she could hear and see everything. All the businesses—Staples, ShopRite, McDonald's, Burlington Coat

Factory—had customer restrooms; and the NYSC gym, where she worked out and took showers, was right behind the McDonald's. She decided to stay another night. She backed her gray Toyota between the back of the building and the fence under the trees. *Secure,* she thought, the same feeling she had after going out on night missions in Afghanistan and making it back through the gate at the outpost. *Secure for now.* She reached behind the passenger seat into the REI shopping bag. Maryann hadn't been completely truthful to Davie. She had his money; it was just in REI merchandise. She had bought clothing, no-rinse bathing wipes, and an Aurelle toothbrush—because of its convenient refillable toothpaste-tube handle and the all-in-one carrying case. She also splurged on an emergency bivy sack to keep her warm on winter nights. In between her thoughts, Warren's burner phone would ring and someone would leave a voice or text message. She listened to each message three times to make sure she got every detail correct for her meeting with Warren.

It was midnight when she finished rewriting her notes. When she looked at the time, she realized she forgot to take the battery out of the phone. As she quickly removed the battery, she realized that in four short hours, she would have her second meeting with Warren. She needed to be alert for the meeting. She didn't trust him; how could she trust a drug dealer? She wondered if she should sleep for a couple hours or stay awake and drink a lot of coffee at the meeting. She looked down at the cell phone battery in her hand and realized she had no alarm to wake her up, so her only option was to stay awake and hope an adrenaline rush would keep her going.

CHAPTER 5

In the morning, Maryann used the no-rinse wipes to wash and get her game face on. She went to the diner early so she could scope it out and pick a table; she used the same skills the CIA had taught her. The diner doors were precisely in the middle of the diner. On the left were all booths; on the right were all tables. The front wall was all windows and booths. The side walls on both sides of the diner were solid, no windows or doors. She chose a table close to the solid wall, with a full view of all the windows and doors. She felt prepared.

At 4:00 a.m., right on time, Warren walked into the diner. He walked straight to the last booth on the left side and motioned to Maryann to join him. *So much for that plan*, she thought. *Looks like the games are starting.*

"Hey, Warren," said Sal, the owner of the diner. "I see you took your favorite booth."

"Good morning, Sal. Yeah, I like this spot. I get to see the comings and goings of Massapequa from here, and now and then I see some of the Massapequa elite in here doing business."

"Are you going to have the usual?" asked Sal.

"Yes, please," replied Warren.

"And your new friend?" Sal asked as Maryann sat down in the booth.

Not sure of what to say, Maryann replied, "I'll have the same, the usual."

"The usual," Sal explained, "is two eggs over easy, hash browns, two sausages, two pancakes, and orange juice and coffee."

"That sounds fine," replied Maryann, but she thought, *That's more food than I eat in a day.*

As Sal walked away, Warren turned his attention to Maryann. "Let me see the messages you got last night."

Maryann gave Warren the paper with her notes:

516798415 Chicago Cubs by 2
6315542398 Seattle Mariners in 4
5167995311 Houston Astros by 3
5162641313 Mets ahead in the 6
5167978213 Oakland A's by 5
5167995410 Oakland A's in 3

"Okay, good. You parked behind the diner, right?"

As Maryann nodded her head, she remembered that there were no windows in the back of the diner, and at 4:00 a.m., most people were asleep in bed.

"As we speak, your car is getting loaded with these products," Warren told her with cold indifference. "You will be making the deliveries."

"How?" Maryann asked.

Just then, Sal walked over to the table and said, "Breakfast is served. Put your papers away and eat."

As Sal walked away, Warren started to explain how. "Each one of these numbers has an address, except the ones that say *in*. *In* means you drop the drugs off at Burns. The numbers are the amount and which port-a-potty to drop the drugs in. In the park, you pick up the money in—" Warren stopped for a moment and then continued, "Well, you already know where you pick up the money, don't you?"

"Yeah, the garbage bin," Maryann replied.

"But what does all this mean?" Maryann asked, gesturing toward her paper of text messages.

"Oakland A's is for oxycodone, Chicago Cubs is for cocaine, Seattle Mariners is for speed, Houston Astros is for heroin, Mets is for marijuana. Every morning we will meet, you will tell me the orders and pay me for the goods from the day before. While we're eating, your car will be loaded with the new products you need to sell. Oh, and starting tomorrow, you pay for breakfast for the both of us. When we get the bill, you put all the cash on the table. I take my cut, Sal gets his for the meals and tips, and the rest is yours."

As they finished their meals, Warren asked, "Any questions?"

Maryann shook her head no.

"Oh, by the way, when you deliver to Burns, the clients coming there to pick up know that they have to pick up pebbles to signify which port-a-potty they are going to. The real reason we ask them to do that is to make sure they are the right people getting the drugs. Most cops will go right to the port-a-potty. If there is a problem with the pickup, you will get a text message."

"From you?" asked Maryann.

"No," replied Warren. "It would be from a spotter. You don't need to know his name."

Warren leaned over closer to Maryann so no one else could hear and said, "Look, bottle lady, you screw up here, I'll put a bullet in your head. All your Special Forces training won't mean shit. Do you understand?" As he spoke, his eyes glared right into Maryann's face, as if looking for an opening to crush her soul.

"I understood everything you said," Maryann said in the toughest tone she could muster. Returning his stare with steely eyes, she continued with anger and confidence, "If I didn't understand what you meant, I would have said so. I won't screw up. This isn't rocket science."

At the end of the meal, a window washer appeared outside and tapped on the window in front of their booth. He was about five feet tall with a slender build and close-cropped hair. Warren seemed to pay no attention to him but smiled at Maryann and said, "We are done here. Start making your deliveries. Customers are waiting."

CHAPTER 6

For the first couple of deliveries, Maryann was a complete wreck, not sure what to expect from the clients. Warren had instructed her on how to make the home deliveries: Knock on the door and say, "Sports tickets delivery." The client would yell back, "Leave them under the mat!" Under the mat, she would find an envelope with the payment money, which she would take out and replace with the drugs. Maryann liked this procedure because she never saw anyone, and she hoped no one saw her.

She wasn't as comfortable with the procedure at Burns Park. Once she put the drugs in the port-a-potties, she was never sure if she was going to get paid. The fate of her predecessors always loomed in the back of her mind, so Maryann decided to change all the Burns Park clients to address clients. She also wondered who and where this spotter was. She figured the spotter was there to protect Warren. If there was a problem, the spotter would turn into a sniper, and she would be the first to get hit. Within a few weeks, she had switched all the park clients to address clients, so no more port-a-potty trans-actions for her.

The 4:00 a.m. breakfast meetings went on for months, and their business had been steadily increasing. Maryann was falling into a routine: Warren's meetings, making deliveries, writing out the text messages. She even found time to go clothes shopping, and she rented an apartment. She often thought every time she walked through her apartment door how great it was to have a comfortable bed and heat and air conditioning compared to living in her car. Maryann was still bringing the entire day's earnings to the meetings. The only problem was that the money no longer fit in her pockets, so she started bringing the cash in a large brown paper bag, the type you get from the large department stores. The night before, in preparation for the meeting and to disguise what they were doing, she would buy clothing—usually men's shirts and pants. Once, she even bought a raincoat.

The week before Christmas, Maryann noticed that Warren was acting differently; he was smiling more and seemed more relaxed. Maryann showed up to their next meeting with a holiday-themed paper bag instead of the usual plain brown.

"Hey, bottle lady." Warren always greeted her that way to get her attention.

And Maryann always just glared at him with a look that said, "Yes, asshole."

"Two things: I noticed that all the Burns clients are now address clients. I like that. Good job. Secondly, I want to give you a Christmas gift." Maryann was a little surprised. She expected Warren to produce some sort of wrapped package on the table, but he just sat there with his hands folded. After a long pause, he said, "Your debt to me is paid off. After working together for six months, I would say that we are now somewhat partners."

"So what does that mean?" Maryann asked.

"It means you can get smaller bags," Warren answered.

They both broke out in laughter, the type that comes deep from your belly. It was Maryann's first laugh in six months. She still feared Warren, but the hairs on the back of her neck didn't stand up as much anymore. She was beginning to feel that Warren wasn't such a creep after all.

"Okay, how much do I bring? I need to know what size bag to buy," Maryann said, smiling at Warren, her new business partner.

Warren started to motion with his hands what the business split was going to be but stopped as Sal came to the booth to ask how everything was.

"Excellent as usual," Warren answered.

"Do you know the 7-Eleven on Merrick Road, by the school?" Sal asked Warren.

Warren looked at Maryann and said, "Isn't that near your apartment?"

35

"Yes," said Maryann, hiding her surprise that he knew where she lived.

Warren looked back at Sal and asked, "Yeah, what's up?"

Sal continued, "They are having cash flow problems and looking for a silent partner."

"You know this guy?" asked Warren.

"Yeah, through the Massapequa Chamber of Commerce," Sal replied. "He wants to expand the store to the lot next to it."

"How much is he looking for?" Warren asked.

"250,000," Sal replied. "I know you know a lot of people. Hopefully, you can help him out."

"I'll see," Warren answered. As Sal walked away, Warren told Maryann, "You should invest in it."

"What do you mean? I don't have that kind of money," Maryann said. "And I don't know anything about a 7-Eleven."

"After a couple months of not having to pay me back, you'll have the money," Warren answered. "And as to running a retail business, Maryann, you are *in* the retail business. Don't worry. 7-Eleven is a franchise. They train you. And remember, this guy wants a *silent* investor to expand the store. Basically, he's just looking for a loan, and you can probably loan it to him as needed and charge him interest or a lower payback for a percentage of the profit for life—your own private annuity."

"Okay, I'll think about it. Let's get back to how much do I bring to our meeting?" Maryann asked.

Warren pointed to himself and said, "Sixty," then he pointed to Maryann and said, "Forty." Just then, there was a tap on the window by the same window washer. Warren, as usual, motioned that the meeting was over and got up and walked toward the door.

Maryann thought, *If this guy is a window washer, how come I've never seen him washing the windows here at the diner?* Then her mind went back to wondering how Warren had found out where she lives. She had been very careful to keep a low profile and used her military training to make sure no one ever followed her home. *Is it possible I hadn't noticed him following me home after a meeting?* She concluded there was no point in guessing; she would just ask him the next morning.

After the holidays, George and Neil finally had time to catch up. They agreed to meet one morning at the Nautilus Diner. Neil arrived first and ordered coffee and bagels, as usual. He waved when he saw George walk through the front door.

"Good morning, Neil. Long time no see," said George.

"Yeah, too long! How were your holidays?" asked Neil.

"Good and peaceful," replied George.

"Are you still jogging at Burns?" asked Neil. "I haven't heard any updates from you in a while about your pebble-potty mystery, so I thought maybe you had retired from running too. Or did Olivia find out you were on a case and ban you from the park?"

"Very funny. No, I'm still running…well, it is more like *walking* lately because of the ice and snow. But it's been quiet there too," replied George. "A little too quiet."

"How so?" asked Neil.

"No activity at all at the port-a-potties—no one picking up pebbles and putting them on the bench. The last activity I saw was in late August, and then one day, they just stopped. You didn't call the guys at the department again, did you?"

"Of course not. I was waiting for the word from you. Let's hope this means the drug drops have stopped."

"They probably just moved on to other communities," George lamented.

"Well, at least it's better for Burns and our community," stated Neil.

"We'll see about that," George said. "I'm not convinced they're gone for good. Maybe they just changed their MO. I'm still keeping my eyes open every day at the park."

As they finished up their breakfast, the subject changed to family and other community topics. When they were done, they planned to meet again in a month, and George promised to contact Neil right away if any suspicious activity started up again.

As Maryann mundanely made her deliveries throughout the day, she kept thinking about Warren's suggestion to invest in the 7-Eleven. *Why does he care how I spend my money? Will I really have that much money in a couple months?* She decided to go check it out, and it turned out to be the highlight of her day. There was a steady stream of people walking in, getting coffees, bagels, donuts, hot dogs, Slurpees. From a retail perspective, the traffic was good, and she could see that expanding the store would make it even better. She decided right then that she would do it.

As Maryann was walking out of the store, she was surprised to see Caroline walk in. She smiled politely at Maryann and then walked to the coffeepots. Caroline had become one of Maryann's every-other-day clients. After the last body search by Jonathan, she had decided it would be smarter to only buy as needed. That way, she didn't have to worry about Jonathan finding a stash in his house.

Maryann wanted to keep her reaction to Caroline to a minimum so no one could tell that they knew each other. She was still preoccupied with her business prospect anyway and walked to the parking lot to see if it would be big enough after the expansion. After only a couple minutes, the front door of the store opened, and Caroline walked past Maryann and stealthily stuffed a note into her hand. The note read: Oakland A's 1 here, 6:00 a.m. Maryann stuffed the note in her pocket and walked back into the 7-Eleven to get some of its famous coffee. With coffee in hand, Maryann stood outside. This time it was to check for any surveillance or security cameras in the area to determine if it was a safe place to make the drop for Caroline the next day.

To the right of the 7-Eleven was a bar—no cameras there. Across the street was a supermarket parking lot and a restaurant—no cameras at those locations. Next to the restaurant was a TD Bank, where Maryann had an account. She didn't see any obvious cameras, but she thought she better check it out to make sure. Across from the bank was a gas station; they definitely had cameras. On the left side of the 7-Eleven was an office building. There were no sign of cameras there either, but she was going to double-check there too.

Maryann walked across the street and into the TD Bank. She asked to see the bank manager because she had done business with her before.

"Hi, Amelia," Maryann said as the bank manager walked up to her.

"Hi, Maryann, what can I do for you?"

"Yesterday, my friend borrowed my car. And when she brought it back, it had a big dent in the back side. She told me she had stopped here and parked out front facing Merrick Road. Do you have cameras for that area so I could see if someone hit my car?"

"No," Amelia said. "We just have cameras for the front door area and, of course, on the inside. But not the area facing Merrick Road."

"Okay, thank you anyway. Bye," Maryann replied.

Maryann left the bank and walked across to the gas station. She got in line to buy a lotto ticket while she checked how far the camera's view was. *Great,* she thought, *it just took in the gas pumps.* The last location to check was the building next to the 7-Eleven. *If there are no cameras there, I'm home free,* she thought.

The parking was all underneath the building, and it was frequently referred to as the building on stilts. Maryann found the manager's office and asked the same question she had asked at the bank. The manager asked if her friend had been going to the 7-Eleven.

"Not sure. I wasn't with her," Maryann replied.

"Well, some people are parking in this lot for 7-Eleven. Your friend is lucky she didn't get towed," the manager said, obviously annoyed by the unauthorized use of their lot.

"Okay, but do you have cameras?" Maryann asked.

"Yes, we do," the manager stated. "We got them because an accident happened in the parking lot, and a big brouhaha developed. Since then, the owner put in cameras to solve those problems and catch vandals. Where did you say your friend parked?"

"In the front, up against the fence facing 7-Eleven," Maryann replied. "It just happened yesterday. Can I see the tape?"

"It is all digital. What time yesterday?" asked the manager.

"In the afternoon," Maryann replied.

As they both looked through the afternoon footage, Maryann could see the camera could only pick up one parking space in the 7-Eleven lot, right next to the fence between the two businesses.

Coast clear, Maryann thought to herself.

"Do you see your car, miss?" the manager asked.

"No," Maryann answered, "but thanks for your help anyway."

As she walked out, Maryann was certain that she could deal at the 7-Eleven and not be picked up on any cameras. But she was only going to do this for Caroline. There was something about Caroline that made Maryann feel comfortable.

Morning finally came around. Warren did his usual routine. For the first time, she saw how much money was involved in Warren's little ring. The sixty-forty split netted Maryann $2,000. After the split was done, Maryann asked her question: "Warren, how did you find out where I live?"

"Easy," Warren replied. "I own Southpoint. In July, your lease application came across my desk, as does every other lease application."

Maryann said "oh," smiled, and left the diner to go meet Caroline at the 7-Eleven. Maryann stood outside the 7-Eleven, away from the cameras. Soon she spotted Caroline riding her mountain bike into the store parking lot. Caroline parked her bike next to where Maryann was standing and then walked inside to buy two large coffees. Her bike had two water bottle holders and a RockBros front frame top tube bag. While Caroline was inside, Maryann unzipped the RockBros bag and stuffed her Oakland A's request in as she withdrew the cash for the merchandise. Maryann started to think, *Is this worth the risk?* She had moved up in the organization, with people working for her to make the drops. Just then, Caroline walked out of the 7-Eleven, smiled at Maryann, and sat down on the bench. As she was pouring the coffee into the water bottles, Maryann said, "Enjoy" and smiled back. The thoughts of risk disappeared.

Warren and Maryann's business had exploded. They were getting calls from out-of-state cartel members for Long Island weed; the profits were unbelievable. They had bought a safe house to store the drugs and split the cash. But Warren warned Maryann not to change her lifestyle, and both promised to make it a practice of living under the radar.

Maryann started to buy commercial real estate like Southpoint. In five months, she owned three apartment complexes with a total of fifty units and was a silent partner in the 7-Eleven. Maryann thought she was becoming an honest business person. Hopefully, she could eventually get out of this criminal enterprise.

The day after St. Patrick's Day, all peace and quiet was shattered. Maryann was going about her normal early morning routine packing the money into the bags when there was what sounded like a knock on the door. Not sure what to do, Maryann stood in silence, then there was another knock on the door. Maryann's hair on the neck stood at attention. Maryann thought, *If I call 911, they are going to ask questions about the bags of money, and they will take eight minutes to get here. I'm dead by then*, she thought. She quickly picked up the phone and dialed Warren's number. As she hit the send button, another knock occurred, then the door broke open. Two men stood in the opening and walked toward her, saying, "Give us the money and we won't kill you." From the tattoos on their necks and faces, she knew they were MS-13. She also knew whatever she did, they would kill her. As they moved closer, Maryann moved backward in the apartment. She reached the wall and was about to panic when Warren ran into the apartment and grabbed one by the neck while shooting the other in the face with a Beretta equipped with silencer. The shot wasn't heard outside the apartment, but the blood made Maryann's apartment look like a Jackson Pollock painting. Warren then wrestled the other man to the ground. As he pinned him to the floor, Warren took out a knife and cut his throat from ear to ear. Maryann gasped as she watched Warren knife the other man to death. Warren stood up and went to hug Maryann, but she pushed him away. Warren looked confused. He was thinking, *I just saved your life. What's wrong?* But as if Warren was on autopilot, he dialed

41

his phone and said, "Hello, Mark, its Warren. I need a vacuum and clean at the apartment complex. You better bring the wet vac. It's a bloody mess. A pipe must have opened somewhere."

Mark replied, "My team will be there in ten."

Warren asked, "Can you make it five? I must relocate the tenant."

"Okay, will be there in five. On my way now," Mark answered.

Warren spotted the bag with the men's clothing and started to take off his shirt and pants that were drenched in blood, dropped them on the MS-13 bodies, and reached for the clothes in the bag. As he was getting dressed, he looked at Maryann and said, "Get some clothes and the money together. I need to take you to another apartment." As they were leaving her apartment, a car drove up and flashed its lights twice. Warren nodded. Maryann couldn't see who it was; the car was too dark. She could only think it was Mark to clean up the mess. Warren and Maryann walked to the last building in the complex, away from the road and other buildings. As Warren tapped the code into the keypad, he said, "There are only four apartments in this building, and they are all vacant because I just had them all refurbished. And I upgraded the alarm system and dead bolt lock on the doors.

Once inside the furnished apartment, Maryann asked, "Who were those people? How did they find me?"

Warren shrugged his shoulder and said, "You must have dropped your guard somewhere."

Maryann shook her head and said no!

Warren said, "Take a shower, get some rest, and we will talk about it in the morning".

As Warren left the apartment, Maryann sat in silence, thinking about every second of what just happened. Then she remembered what her mother told her when she was around sixteen; it was that God gave women an extra sense to protect themselves: a creep detector. Her mother said, "Most women get into trouble when they don't listen to the hairs on their neck. Now that you are becoming a woman and I can't be with you all the time, use God's extra gift to protect yourself." She thought, *I should have called Warren as soon as my hairs stood up. Maybe the outcome would have been different.*

When Warren got home, he spoke to his brother, Steven Santangelo. Steven was his own man, confident and comfortable in who he was. He was an extremely bright IT guy who was five foot eight with close-cropped hairstyle and a smile that goes ear to ear.

"Steven," Warren said, "we'll need an exit strategy like a prepper, and we need a place to go to that is secure and off the grid like an eagle's nest."

"Okay, all the plans will be under the file Eagle's Nest, but how is Maryann?" asked Steven.

"She is shaken up but okay," replied Warren.

In the morning, Warren and Maryann met at the safe house. After discussing the usual morning business and the split, Maryann said to Warren, "Aren't we going to discuss the damn elephant in the room? Who were those guys?"

"Maryann," replied Warren in a pissed voice, "stop it. You know damn well who those guys were. They were MS-13. My concern is," continued Warren in a more concerned tone, "what did you do, what guard did you drop to bring attention to yourself and now me? Have you personally taken on any new clients?"

"Not new, but Caroline started to buy again," Maryann stated.

"At the park?" Warren asked.

"No, at the 7-Eleven," Maryann answered.

"For how long?" Warren asked.

"A couple weeks," replied Maryann.

"She may have been the connection," said Warren. "She may have been buying from them and stopped and started buying from you. MS-13 may have caught you supplying her."

"No, it couldn't be her. She is a one-pill-a-day or every-oth-er-day client," Maryann continued. "By the way, thank you for last night."

"No problem," replied Warren. "After all, I couldn't let those thugs hurt my partner. It would be bad for business." He smiled at her and moved close to her to give her a hug. Maryann sensed he needed a hug and let it happen.

But like every other business, when competitors find out how much money you're making, they start moving in on your business. One day in May, Warren got a phone call from his Mexico cartel connection asking to meet with Warren and Maryann at Pilgrim State Hospital, a closed psychiatric hospital. Warren said, "No, thanks. If you want to meet with us, we will do it at the Nautilus Diner, our regular breakfast place."

Maryann overheard the conversation and asked, "What's going on? We never go for breakfast at the Nautilus."

Warren replied, "I'm not comfortable with this. At four in the morning, cops stop in at the Nautilus for some food, and they stop by the—"

Maryann finished his sentence, "The 7-Eleven for coffee."

"We will be safer there," Warren said. After a pause, he continued, "Maryann, I've been getting calls or feelers from other cartel organizations. You know the guys from out of state buying the Long Island weed—they want to buy us out. I have always said no because most of them are MS-13, who are reckless and ruthless. Most of them end up in jail, so we didn't have to worry about them coming after us. Besides, if I ever sold to an out-of-state cartel or MS-13, there would be world war III with the local MS-13."

"So who is this meeting with?" asked Maryann.

"Their boss and my direct contact," answered Warren.

CHAPTER 7

The meeting had been set up for the next morning at the Nautilus. As Maryann walked into the diner, Warren was already there, sitting at the table where he and Maryann had their first meeting. As Maryann sat down, Warren whispered to her, "The two visitors are here. Be still and listen. We will talk later."

The visitors walked up to Warren and Maryann's table and said, "Warren and Maryann, we presume." They sat down at the table without waiting for an invitation. It was undeniable who they were. The markings on their faces and necks said it all: MS-13. The hair on Maryann's neck stood straight up, her mother's warning. She thought, *These are not the people I want to do business with.*

"We just ordered breakfast. Do you want to order anything?" Warren asked as calmly and politely as if he were dealing with fellow businessmen from the chamber of commerce.

"Sure," said the taller of the two visitors. Warren motioned to the waiter.

When the waiter approached, the taller visitor turned and said, "We'll have the same as they are having and two cups of coffee." As he turned, Warren saw the gun under his left arm.

"Let's get down to business. I'm Ángel, and this is Juan. We were sent by the cartel to help you expand the business because according to them, you don't want to."

"Let's not get off on the wrong foot," Warren stated. "What the cartel wants to do is great, but you need an infrastructure of people and transportation to move that amount of product successfully. I told them, time and time again, I only move product with trusted, vetted people. That cuts down on lost product and time in jail."

"The cartel thinks you are stalling," Juan stated in a low but angry voice.

"I don't care if you think I am stalling," Warren shot back with a bit more attitude. "I have done business with the cartel for ten years without one problem. If you want to lose product and go into business with unvetted people, you can do that, but you'll end up with more heat on your operations and jeopardize everything the cartel and I have built."

Clearly the conversation wasn't going well. Just then, a third person walked into the diner. "Mr. Diaz!" Warren shouted. Warren stood up, and they hugged like long-lost brothers. Maryann could see that Mr. Diaz was as tall as Warren, but Warren was a medium-size build, and Mr. Diaz was huge compared to Warren. Mr. Diaz was all muscle. Maryann suspected Diaz would use his build to intimidate people. Mr. Diaz was the cartel's direct representative and the MS-13 boss Warren had been dealing with for the past decade.

Mr. Diaz turned to Ángel and Juan and said, "Gentlemen, I'll take this from here. Don't you ever disrespect Mr. Warren or Ms. Maryann, do you understand?" His words came out like a machete blade falling on their shoulders. Ángel and Juan nodded their heads in agreement and left the table.

"Warren and Maryann, we mean no disrespect," said Mr. Diaz. "We need to grow, and we understand your concerns. You have been good to us. We don't want a war on our hands over territories and neighborhoods."

Warren quickly understood what the meeting was really about: staking claims to neighborhoods and whom you could do business with.

Then Warren said, "Mr. Diaz, thank you for your kindness and directness. Can Maryann and I get back to you tomorrow morning with those answers?"

"Yes, of course," Mr. Diaz replied. He shook Warren's hand, smiled at Maryann, and left. He got into his car and had a little heart-to-heart with Ángel and Juan.

"Listen, you assholes. That man and woman control all of Long Island and half of the city, and not once have they shown up on the

DEA radar. If they want to fight, your heads will be the first to roll in the streets. Warren may not be MS-13, but he can be one mean bastard. Enough to be feared by the cartel and should be by MS-13. The way you were going about this would have caused a war—one that we would have lost."

"But he's gay!" shouted Juan. Diaz slapped him so hard, his face started bleeding.

"What the fuck does that matter? You think a gay guy doesn't know how to fight and protect what's his? You go near these two again, I will kill you myself. Now get the fuck out of my car."

Maryann started laughing.

"What is so funny?" asked Warren.

"I can read lips," said Maryann, "and your friend Mr. Diaz is giving Ángel and Juan a hard time."

"What is he saying?"

Maryann relayed the conversation to Warren and then asked, "Why do they fear you?"

Warren answered, "Wow, those two guys are in trouble."

Then Maryann moved close to Warren and said quietly, "What the hell is going on?"

Warren replied, "We have been asked to name the towns, villages, and neighborhoods we want to continue to do business in and give the rest to them. We have twenty-four hours to tell them, or world war III will start."

"What does that mean for us?" Maryann asked.

"It means we are going to scale back our operations into areas that we know well and will bring less attention to us," Warren said. "The problem with these guys is they think brute strength will always win the day. Their way of communicating is a chop of a machete, which will bring on more heat. Our way of business is white-glove treatment, which doesn't attract the attention of the cops."

"So what the hell is going on, and what are we going to do?" asked Maryann.

"Most of our good business is east of Meadowbrook Parkway, south of the LIE, out to the outlets in Riverhead. Look, the city is ready to blow. Kids are dying from the shit MS-13 is pushing.

The cops are looking to arrest anyone involved. I'm happy we are no longer going to be involved. West of Meadowbrook and the North Shore, we have to give up something. The area I want will give us a good income and eventually give you an excellent income."

Maryann felt a bomb had just dropped when Warren said "and eventually give you an excellent income." "Warren, what do you mean? I never wanted to go into this business. You forced me into this business, remember?" Maryann said with anxiety and anger in her voice.

"Yeah right," Warren responded with a pissed attitude. "I forced you out of living in your car to a beautiful apartment and gave you a 40 percent ownership in my business that has enabled you to buy real estate and other retail businesses. Give me a break."

"Maryann," Warren said in a softer tone, "I have been in this business for a decade. How long can you stay under the radar and out of jail? Don't worry. I'm not leaving tomorrow. I'll be with you for a while." Maryann finally took a breath. Warren, for the first time, put his hand on hers and said, "It will be okay." He smiled at her, paid the bill, and left the diner.

Warren had never expected to get into the drug business. Like most people, it wasn't until he had no other means to support himself. He had been wounded in the war by a high-velocity bullet that went right through his left shoulder. The numerous surgeries to remove the dead or damaged tissue in his shoulder led to a lot of pain. When he could no longer get prescription painkillers, he turned to the street to get some relief. After he was caught in a sting operation of Wall Street brokers, the Securities and Exchange Commission revoked his securities license. The cartel thought Warren had ratted them out and sent people to rough him up. Warren had defeated each of them, even with a bum shoulder. That was when the cartel offered him a territory. And much like his job offer to Maryann, it was one he couldn't afford to refuse.

After leaving Maryann at the diner, Warren got into his car and immediately made a call to his brother. "Steven, hi, it's Warren."

"Yes, I know. I have caller ID, remember? How did the meeting go?"

"Not good," Warren said. "It's prepper time."

"Seriously? By the way, how did Maryann do?" asked Steven.

"Seriously, you're asking me about Maryann when I'm telling you it's prepper time?" replied Warren. "Steven, we've talked about this before. We got a month to get everything done and move. Dust off your notes, update them if you need to, but we need to make a decision quickly. See you at home shortly."

Warren and Steve's house had been rebuilt after Hurricane Sandy. It was the last house on the block. The back of the house faced the Great South Bay, and from the backyard, you could see the Jones Beach water tower. To the right of the home was a canal, where he docked his boat. When the hurricane hit, it had brought six feet of water into the house. When the water rescinded, it left everything else it brought in: dead animals, clothing, furniture, toys, a small car, and enough sand to make their own Jones Beach.

"Are you sure we can't stay here?" Steven asked.

"Positive," Warren answered, and from the tone of his voice, Steven knew there was not a doubt in his mind. "Steven," Warren continued, "you know these people aren't the type who will leave us alone. I knew this day would come. It's here, and we have to move."

"What are we going to do with the house?" asked Steven.

"When the time comes, I'll sell it to Maryann. She's going to need a place like this, with all the protections we've added."

"Can I give you the list tomorrow?" Steven asked. "I need to start dinner now."

"Sure," Warren said, smiling and laughing. "But tomorrow, call Bob the real estate guy and tell him to value all the properties and what they are worth in a quick sale. Tell him I want two numbers: what they are worth if I wait for the right buyer and what they are worth in a quick sale."

"You mean that really tall guy from the chamber, Robert?" asked Steven.

"Yes," answered Warren.

"Got it," Steven answered. "See you at dinnertime."

CHAPTER 8

The next morning at the diner was tense. Mr. Diaz showed up by himself, minus his pit bulls, Ángel and Juan. The waiter served coffee, and they got right down to business.

"Warren," Mr. Diaz began, "have you decided the areas you want?"

"Yes," answered Warren. "East of Meadowbrook Parkway and south of the LIE to the Riverhead outlets. You get the city and all else."

"I agree, but it can't go past the Sagtikos Parkway," replied Mr. Diaz.

Warren answered in one word, "Unacceptable." His tone let Mr. Diaz know it was firm.

"Warren, please. The Brentwood area is their home turf. They are going to sell there, and the problems will start."

"Which you will have to fix," Warren replied, again his tone saying more than his words.

After a long period of silence, Mr. Diaz proposed, "Warren, we can carve out Brentwood from east of Sagtikos Parkway, south of the LIE, north of the Southern State Parkway, west of Route 111. Plus to keep the peace, I'll give a commission of 5 percent."

Warren shot back, "10 percent. We are losing the college."

Maryann had been sitting there quietly the whole time. She had never seen Warren talk or act like this before, but then again, from the moment she met Mr. Diaz, the hairs on the back of her neck had been at full attention.

After a long pause, Mr. Diaz replied, "They won't like it, but I'll make it stick. You have a deal." Just then, Warren's cell phone rang. It was Steven.

"Warren," he said, "there are a lot of people roaming around the house."

"Activate the panels and get to the safe room," Warren said. "I will be there shortly." Warren looked directly at Mr. Diaz, got close to his face, and said, "These people better not be yours." Diaz started to react defensively and quickly understood why the cartels had told him not to take Warren on—because he didn't stand a chance against him.

As Warren got up, he looked at Maryann and said, "Let's go." When they got outside, Warren told her, "Go to the safe house, not to your apartment, and stay there until I call you." Warren jumped into the Escalade and flew down East Shore Drive toward his home.

When Warren got home, no one was around, but the house was in full lockdown mode. To enter the property without getting shot, he had to enter a code into his cell phone twice. As soon as he entered the code the second time, the lights came back on, and the computerized guns disappeared from sight. Warren unlocked the front door and went to the safe room, where Steven had been waiting. As they met, they hugged, and Warren asked, "Were the cameras working?"

"Yes," said Steven. "We got pictures of them."

Warren took one look at them and said, "It's Juan." He picked up his cell phone and called Mr. Diaz. "Diaz, you got a problem. Juan was just at my home. Are you going to take care of this, or will I? And if your answer is *you* will, I will need proof. Do you understand?" Diaz could tell by Warren's tone that he was pissed and dead serious. If he didn't take care of Juan right away, it could ignite world war III in the drug community, and Diaz knew that his bosses would blame him.

"Warren, I understand. I will deal with Juan immediately, and I will bring proof," Diaz replied. Diaz realized this needed to be handled in a way that his bosses didn't hear about it. Diaz's bosses had told him to cut a deal with Warren, not kill him. Warren was too valuable to them. No one could fully explain the importance of Warren. Whenever Diaz asked why Warren was so important, his bosses would only say, "You don't need to know. Just understand that he is very valuable to our organization."

Diaz called Ángel. "Do you know where Juan is?"

Ángel replied, "Not sure, why?"

Diaz replied, "Find him immediately and meet me at Pilgrim State. And, Ángel, don't fuck this up! We need to meet up within the hour. At the water tower. Do you understand?"

"Yes, Mr. Diaz," Ángel replied.

The Pilgrim State water tower was located in a wide-open field shaped like a horseshoe. Looking south from the water tower, there was a one-lane service road; this road was the only access road to the water tower. Looking north, east, and west from the tower, you were surrounded by large leafy trees. This made it almost impossible to see the tower from the other side. Simply put, it was a perfect place to hold a private meeting.

"Ángel, do you have Juan?" asked Mr. Diaz.

"Please, sir," answered Ángel, trying to prevent the inevitable.

Diaz interrupted him, "Bring him forward. Did you remember to bring the burlap sack?"

"Yes, sir," answered Ángel, realizing there was nothing he could possibly do to help his friend.

Ángel and his crew crowded closer to the tower to hear what Mr. Diaz was going to say to Juan.

"Juan," Mr. Diaz started, "you broke rule number 1. Any conflicts between cliques that require a resolution are handled by senior leadership. Correct?"

Juan nodded his head. "Yes."

"I personally told you not to touch Warren, and you went to his home without senior leadership authorization. The cartel can't have cliques moving about in conflict with other cliques. But I guess you feel you are above senior leadership."

Juan shook his head no.

"Juan," Diaz continued, "senior leadership has made a decision. Your disloyalty must be punished." As Mr. Diaz was talking, he slowly pulled a gun out of his pocket and slowly screwed a silencer onto it. He pointed it at Juan and said, "Good night and goodbye." *CLICK*.

As Juan fell to the ground, Diaz told Ángel to put him in the sack and put him in the back of Diaz's car. While Ángel was putting the sack containing Juan's lifeless body into the car, Diaz called Warren.

"Warren, this is Diaz. I have your proof."

"Good. Where do you want to meet? Warren asked.

"Gilgo," stated Diaz.

"Fine," answered Warren. "See you in an hour."

Warren hung up the phone, turned to Steven, and said, "Call the vacuum-and-cleanup crew and tell them we have a meeting with MS-13 and I need protection."

Steven asked, "Is this going to be like the shootout at the OK Corral?"

"Only if they start it," answered Warren.

Warren's crew got to Gilgo fifteen minutes after the call; ahead of Diaz, they set themselves up strategically along Ocean Parkway. Warren parked his Escalade on the bay side of the road, took a 9mm gun from the center console, and then called Steven while he waited.

"Hey, Steven, I'm going to leave the phone on so you hear what's happening. If this doesn't go down as I expect it, I want you to get Maryann. Don't call her. You have to go to the safe house to get her. Explain to her what happened and take her to our house to protect her. Don't let her go to her apartment at Southpoint. It won't be safe. Take the Hummer. It will protect both of you until you get back to the house. Once you get back home, go into lockdown mode. Tell her everything and come up with a plan. Once you are back at the house, go to the safe. There is an envelope in there with her name on it. Give it to her, tell her to read it, and then plan your response. Steven, guide her as you have guided me. Do you understand?" Warren asked.

"I hope it doesn't come to this, but yes, I understand. But I have to say, I don't like it," Steven replied.

"Steven, a car is coming," Warren stated. "It's pulling up behind me." Warren picked up the walkie-talkie to talk to his crew. "Okay, guys, heads up. Let's be ready for anything and everything. If they start anything, we need to finish it."

After each of the crew members responded with either a "ten-four" or "copy that," Warren set the walkie-talkie down and watched in his rearview mirror.

The car stopped right behind Warren's. When the door opened, Warren readied his gun. Diaz stepped out, holding his hands up in the air. He opened his jacket so Warren could see that there was no weapon on him. Diaz turned around to show Warren he had nothing in his back belt area either. At this point, Warren got out of his car and walked over to Diaz.

"Where is the proof?" Warren asked.

"The trunk," answered Diaz.

They both walked to the back of Diaz's car, and Diaz hit the button to open the trunk. As Warren raised the trunk, a light went on, and Warren could see Juan's dead body. The back of his head was gone; the bullet had entered from his face and exited through the back of his head. It was a bloody mess.

"Are we good?" Diaz asked.

"For now, but I want what I outlined this morning," Warren answered in the same dead-serious, pissed-off tone as before.

"10 percent override on the college territory plus the Brentwood area," replied Diaz.

"Yes, and this better not happen again," Warren warned.

"Understood," Diaz replied, and then he asked, "See you tomorrow?"

"No," Warren stated firmly. "Give me a few days. I need to fit this all together."

"I understand," Diaz answered.

Warren got into his car and drove off, while Diaz dumped Juan's body onto the ground and began to drag it into the swampy area off the parkway.

As Warren drove away, he picked up the walkie-talkie and told his men to stand down but to watch how Diaz was disposing the body. "Only leave your secure positions once Diaz has left. Guys, I owe you dinner tomorrow night. Nautilus Diner at six."

"Ten-four."

"Ten-four."

"Ten-four."
"Ten-four."
"Ten-four."
"Ten-four."

As Warren was driving home, he called out to Steven, "Are you still here?"

Steven asked, "How did it go? Once you left the car, I couldn't hear what was going on, so what happened?

"We got what we asked for, but we can discuss this later. I still want you to go to the safe house and get Maryann. Bring her to the house so I can discuss some things with her. After that, you and I need to discuss Eagle's Nest."

"Agreed," said Steven.

By the time Warren got back home, Steven and Maryann were waiting for him in the living room. Warren walked in and sat down next to Maryann. "Maryann, the reason I wanted you to go to the safe house was that I know you don't have any way of protecting yourself at your apartment, even though the owner has hired the very best security detail on the island," Warren said with a smile.

"Yeah, right, but I can take care of myself," Maryann said with a bit of an attitude. "Don't treat me like a princess. I have more military training than most men in this country."

"Maryann," Warren said, giving the attitude right back to her, "stop the shit. MS-13 doesn't fight using the Marquess of Queensberry rules or the UN convention. They fight, in the words of Barack Obama, 'If they bring a knife to a fight, we bring a gun.' MS-13 will use unconventional ways to get to you and me. But I think the problem is solved—for now. Come into the kitchen and sit. Let me explain what happened tonight."

When they got into the kitchen, Warren continued, "Those guys who attacked my house were being led by Juan, who is no longer with us. Diaz saw to that. To make amends for what Juan did, Diaz has agreed to our terms—east of Meadowbrook Parkway and south of the LIE to the Riverhead outlets, except for the Brentwood area. We get a 10 percent override on sales in that area and the college. Diaz will hold the peace as long as he can. Going forward, I think we have a good ten years before the shit starts again or Diaz won't or can't control things. This means two things." Warren raised his index finger to signify his first point. "One, you need to invest all the profits in the next five to six years in other legitimate businesses." Warren raised his index finger and his middle finger together to make sure Maryann was following as he continued, "Two, you need to call Black Ops in Idaho tomorrow. Mention my name and tell them you need a security analyst. They will evaluate your situation, tell you what you need and what it will cost, and will get it done all under the radar."

"I think I've heard of these guys—in Afghanistan. They did black ops. How do you know them?" asked Maryann.

"They were part of my team," Warren replied.

"Not in the Mideast?" blurted Maryann.

"No. Different war, little girl," replied Warren. Maryann let that last comment slip by. She began to realize that there was a lot more to Warren than she ever realized. She stared at him as if she were giving him an MRI to figure him out.

"Maryann!" Warren yelled. "Are you still with us?"

"Yes, yes," Maryann replied. "Sorry. What is our next step?"

"Tomorrow, after our usual meeting at the diner, start looking for businesses or investments that throw off cash." Warren got up and gestured for Maryann to get up too. "Okay, see you tomorrow morning at four."

Maryann laughed. "You do know tomorrow is here and four o'clock is in three hours, right?"

Warren smiled as they walked to the door. "Right. See you in three hours. Here's the number for Black Ops, in case I forget to give it to you after our meeting." Warren took a business card from his wallet and gave it to Maryann. As he closed the door, Warren called out, "Okay, Steven, it's time for you to brief me on Eagle's Nest."

"Where is it?" Warren asked.

"Idaho," Steven replied. "Northern Idaho, to be more precise. It is the top ninety acres of Katha Road in Bonners Ferry. There are four things that I think make it a prepper's dream location. One, it has a grass landing strip for a STOL aircraft. Two, it has four abandoned silver mines—one that hasn't been fully explored yet. And third, there are two homes on the property already, and the main house already has a safe room. The property has space to build at least four more houses without affecting the environment. Four, our only neighbor is the US Forest Service. We can get the contract to cut the dead wood trees off the property to be used for heating or to sell to the log cabin or lumber industry.

"Okay," Warren said. "What's the downside?"

"The downside is," Steven paused, looked at Warren, and said, "remember, when we started this evaluation, we put security at the top—the property had to be defensible, the location had to sustain us—and Black Ops recommended this for us."

"Okay, what the hell is the downside?" Warren asked again, getting a little annoyed.

"The nearest town, Bonners Ferry, has 2,500 people, and it is thirty-five minutes away. This property is way off the grid. The nearest NYC-type nightlife is two hours away. However, the nightlife in Canada is only thirty minutes away. Walmart and Dollar Tree are only thirty minutes away, in Ponderay."

"What's the main house like?" asked Warren.

"The main house is designed like an upside-down *Y*," Steven answered as he began to draw a picture. "The right leg of the *Y* is longer than the left because it has a two-car garage, which leads into the house. As you enter the house through the garage, you pass a large pantry, then you enter the expansive kitchen with a breakfast nook. The stem part of the *Y* is the family room. The whole house has a lot of windows to see the wildlife. The first floor also has a library and two half baths. The second floor has three bedrooms, two full baths, and an office that is large enough to have security screens covering each view of the property. Cell service is excellent, as is the internet, by the way."

Warren sat quietly as Steven pointed out all the features of the house. "The third floor is a glass-enclosed porch. You need to use the elevator to get to it, but it gives you a 360-degree view of the surrounding areas. Below the garage and the first floor is the safe room and a root cellar. The elevator also goes down into the basement next to the safe room, but you can lock it to the first floor or the upper floors if you go into a lockdown scenario. The second house is more like a guest cottage—two bedrooms, a kitchen, one and a half bathrooms, a den or living room, and a fireplace all on one floor."

Warren still didn't say anything, so Steven continued, "The property has a huge barn for animals, a well, wind power, hydropower, solar panels, a generator, and a woodshed the size of a small barn. The price includes all equipment, tools, and furnishings. And the airstrip has its own equipment pole barn."

"Okay, very interesting," Warren asked, "but what about the abandoned mines?"

"Good question," Steven said. "I thought that those mine tunnels would give us great cover for traveling to and from the houses. They can be used as safe rooms for the other house, or we could build out the long unexplored mine tunnel into an underground bunker."

"What did Black Ops say about the underground bunker?" Warren asked.

"They said they first have to check the tunnel to see how solid it is before committing to doing it, but in theory, it is achievable," Steven replied.

"When can it be ready?" Warren asked.

"The property is on the market now," replied Steven. "As to the bunker, I would have to ask for a security evaluation then construction cost and delivery time."

"What is the price of the house and property?" Warren asked.

"880,000. With the improvements that Black Ops said we needed based on our requirements, not counting the bunker, 1 million.

"What do you think?" Warren asked.

"I think it is exactly what we asked for," replied Steven.

"That's not what I'm asking you. Have you seen it?" asked Warren.

"Yes," replied Steven.

"What was your gut reaction? Was it too far-off the radar?" Warren asked.

Almost immediately, Steven answered back, "Yes, too far-off the radar. There is nothing to do but work, eat, and sleep."

"Okay," said Warren, "get on the phone with Black Ops and tell them our concerns. Maybe we are missing something. Ask specifically where the fun is, how far away and how often. They know us, Steven. I feel they would want to point us in the right direction. It might not be a bad idea to party only in Canada and figure out different routes home. I see online that the Best Western has a casino in Bonners Ferry. How close is that?"

"Depends. About twenty-six minutes, but I don't think there is any action there."

"Copy that," Warren answered. "I need to get some rest. I need to get up in an hour. Good night."

CHAPTER 9

When Warren and Maryann took their seats at the diner, Sal came running over with a coffeepot and said, "Warren, thank you for investing in that 7-Eleven! My friend really appreciated it." Warren smiled but said nothing. When Sal walked away and was out of earshot, Warren turned to Maryann and asked, "Did you invest?"

"Yes. I listened to your advice and did my *own* research and started to invest in legitimate businesses," answered Maryann.

"Smart woman," said Warren.

Breakfast came and then the tap on the window by the window washer; only this time, Maryann recognized who he was. In the past, the window washer had concealed his identity with a baseball cap or hoodie that covered his face. But this time the hat was gone, and as he tapped the window, he looked in. All these months, it had been Steven who was stocking her car. She thought to herself, *Looks like drugs are a family affair.* Then she thought, *Warren seems to be more relaxed, and Steven is showing his face. Maybe these guys trust me. Is that good or bad for me?*

Just then, Warren started to talk, but Maryann didn't seem to be listening. He raised his voice a little and said, "Earth to Maryann!"

Maryann replied, "Massapequa to Warren."

"We are going to need to meet up with Diaz to solidify our deal with him and the cartel. Are you available tomorrow night to meet at the Nautilus?"

"Yes, I think so," replied Maryann.

"Okay, I'll call him right now to set it up."

"Good idea," Maryann answered. "The quicker we get this deal under control, the better for us. MS-13 will probably be drawing attention to them, which is less attention on us."

"Hello, Diaz, this is Warren. I'm calling to set up a meeting tomorrow night at the Nautilus Diner, just you, to finalize everything. You understand?...Good. Seven thirty tomorrow night." Warren looked back at Maryann and said, "It's set, and I'll see you later at South Merrick to do the split." South Merrick Road was the safe-house address. It was the only house on the north side of the street. Trees covered the front yard of the house, bordered by the parking lots of two different buildings that faced Merrick Road. The businesses, a physical therapist and a walk-in clinic, created a lot of traffic and parking on the north side of the street (the same side as the safe house), which brought no attention to the house. And the neighbors on the south side of the street were happy to have everyone park on the safe-house side of the road.

As Warren and Maryann left the diner together, Warren called Steven on his cell phone. "Hey, any answer from Black Ops?" Warren asked.

"No," answered Steven. "I just sent them an email, but remember, there is a time difference. There aren't many people up at five a.m. New York time."

"Okay, okay, got your point," Warren answered.

As Maryann was walking to her car, she turned and looked at Warren and asked, "Why couldn't we do the meeting tonight with Diaz? I'd like to get this over with and settled."

"Right, good idea, but I have other plans. I promised to buy dinner for a bunch of guys," Warren answered. "And you should come."

"No, thanks. Dinner with a bunch of guys doesn't sound like a fun time. Who are these guys anyway?" Maryann asked.

"No! You must come because they are my QRF, and eventually they will be your QRF. So you must meet and bond with them."

"Your quick reaction force? Who are these guys? Are they former military?" Maryann asked.

"Yes, they are guys I served with. You know, you ask a lot of questions," Warren answered.

"You invited me, so I have questions," Maryann continued. "By the way, I have another question," Maryann paused. "What time and where?"

"Nautilus at six p.m. Are you going to come?"

"See you at six. Bye," Maryann replied.

Around four thirty that afternoon, Maryann started to get ready for dinner at the Nautilus. As she was pulling on her pants, she looked up and saw the floral-print tube dress hanging in her closet. She thought, *What the hell. It's going to be a warm summer night, and I'm feeling good and a little sexy.* As she pulled the tight, stretchy fabric over her curves, she began to feel like a woman for the first time in many years.

That evening, when she walked into the Nautilus, heads turned; no one had ever seen Maryann dressed up. They were used to seeing her—or not seeing her—dressed in baggy men's pants, an oversize shirt, and an army jacket. It was a great outfit if you want to go unnoticed. Tonight she wanted to be noticed, and she was noticed. She walked over to Warren, who was standing around with his crew, cracking jokes. He hadn't seen her arrive.

Maryann said, "Hey, Warren, this must be your QRF. So are you going to introduce me?"

"Oh, yeah, guys, this is Maryann. She is my partner and friend. Be nice to her," Warren said.

At that moment, Evan came over and asked everyone to sit down so he could start taking their orders. Warren sat at the head of the table, with Steven to his right. At the opposite end of the table, one of the guys pulled out a chair and said to Maryann, "Sit here." Maryann smiled and sat down directly across from Warren. Briefly, her eyes met his, and she knew from his look that he liked what he saw. She thought to herself, *The dress was the right choice.*

"Hey, Warren," Billy yelled out, "have you heard from your Aunt Rock Mama?"

The entire table laughed, and Warren answered, "Yes, and she is hard at work, making those diamond packets."

Then Billy turned to Maryann and said, "Maryann—your name is Maryann, right?" She nodded, and he asked, "How did you meet Warren?"

Maryann wasn't prepared for that question, nor did she really want to tell a guy she just met the whole story. So she turned the question back to him. "How do *you* know Warren?"

"Warren and all the guys here go back to Operation Desert Shield in the Gulf. He was our platoon leader. He kept us alive and safely brought us all home," Billy answered.

"Sounds like you guys have some good wartime buddy stories to tell," Maryann said, trying to get some info from Billy.

Billy replied, "Some of the stories are still classified and can't be told. And the others, well, I'll tell you some other time."

"What do you do now?" Maryann asked.

"Independent insurance adjuster. I investigate claims—worker compensation, auto claims, liability claims, like slips and falls. Warren set me up with my first contract. Here's my card."

Maryann looked at the card and said, "Your company's name is Shield Investigations. Good name." Maryann smiled at Billy.

"Yeah," Billy replied. "I named my company after Operation Desert Shield. I also think that most of the people I do the investigations for are hoping my investigation shields them from liability or a lawsuit."

"Good play on words," Maryann stated and smiled again. "Has that ever happened? Have any of your investigations shielded someone from the claim?"

"Yeah, a couple times. One woman who had broken her tooth after she bit into almond-nut ice cream tried to sue. I found out it was a temporary crown, and her dentist had told her not to have anything very hot or cold. The case was settled for a container of vanilla almond ice cream, the woman's favorite, but the container wasn't shipped until her dentist said it was okay to eat. Another case," Billy went on, "was a worker-compensation case where the employee came to work on a Monday saying he had hurt himself at work on Friday. The owner of the firm told me they have strict rules—if you think you're hurt, you must notify management immediately or no later than the end of the workday so they could get the employee the proper medical attention. The owner felt for sure it was a fraudulent claim, and he was right—the employee got hurt playing baseball on

Saturday by sliding into a second base. But the comp board didn't care. They paid the employee anyway."

"Comp board?" Maryann asked.

"Oh, that's worker compensation board, the people who hear cases for injured-employee compensation claims," Billy explained.

"Oh," said Maryann.

"So how did you meet Warren?" Billy asked again. This time Maryann was prepared.

"Warren and I own rental property together," Maryann stated. *It is true*, she thought. *The safe house is a property we own together. It* could *be rented.* "And he's helping me with some other business investments I'm thinking about," she added.

"Warren does have a good business mind," Billy said.

Evan came with the food, and the table went quiet as everyone started eating. When the conversation picked up again, Maryann got to know a few of the other guys and heard more of their stories. She discovered that Warren had helped out every one of them in one way or another. At the end of the night, Warren went to the end of the table and sat down next to Maryann.

"Did you have fun?" Warren asked.

Maryann said, "Yes, they are a great group of guys. Are they all from your platoon?"

"Yes, all but Steven," replied Warren. "And you," Warren continued, "clean up quite well. That dress looks great on you."

"Thank you," Maryann said with a smile.

As they walked out together, Warren said, "Remember, Diaz tomorrow night. And please don't wear this type of outfit. Wear your regular clothes."

"Got it. All business," Maryann replied.

"Come on, Steven. We have to go," Warren called out.

"Good night," Maryann said to Steven and Warren.

"Good night," they both shouted back.

CHAPTER 10

Wednesday began, as usual, with Warren and Maryann meeting at the diner at 4:00 a.m., and then Maryann left to do her deals. Then she showed up at 7-Eleven to check on the store and to supply Caroline with her special needs. This time, instead of just ordering a one-day fix, Caroline ordered two. Maryann thought that was odd, but she didn't think too much about it; her mind was preoccupied with the meeting with Diaz. To be honest, she was a little concerned about the outcome. The rest of the day seemed to move slowly, until the appointed hour came to meet with Diaz.

"Seven thirty at the Nautilus, right? Is Diaz here?" Maryann asked as she sat down.

"Nope," replied Warren.

A second later, Diaz pulled into the parking lot; he got out of his car and started walking toward the diner's front door with a small binder in his hand.

"Is he by himself?" Maryann asked.

"He better be," replied Warren. "This meeting is by invitation only."

Diaz quickly made it to the table and said "good evening" to Warren and Maryann. As he sat down, he said, "Let's get right to business." He opened his binder and took out a piece of paper titled "The Agreement." The rest of the document wasn't in English.

Warren pointed to the document and said, "Farsi."

"Yes," Diaz replied.

Warren put on his glasses and began reading the document, and Maryann watched as his lips moved. She tried to read it too but could only make out some of the words, which she remembered from her military language training.

After a long period of silence, Warren looked up and said, "The geography is good. It is as we agreed to, minus the Brentwood area and the college plus our 10 percent. Two questions: what do you estimate the 10 percent override to us to be, and how will the cartel supervise or control this agreement?"

Diaz replied, "To question one, 5 million the first year. To the second question, we will be the supplier. If they violate the agreement, we'll shut them down and reorganize their leadership." From Diaz's tone of voice, the cartel wasn't about to take lightly any move that would break this agreement.

Warren looked at Diaz for what seemed a long time. He took off his glasses, slowly put them away, and looked back at Diaz and said, "We have an agreement."

"Good," said Diaz.

Warren looked at Maryann and said, "Let's go. We have work to do." As they walked out of the diner, Warren's cell rang. He looked at his phone and said, "It's Billy. Hey, Billy, what's up?"

"Remember I told you I had to go in for that operation at the VA?" Billy asked.

"Yes," said Warren.

"I just found out that they don't have the money to do the operation. Something about a government shutdown or something like that." The more Billy spoke, the more Warren detected Billy's stress increasing.

"Okay, Billy. I got this. Please relax. Stress is going to kill you. You have an abdominal hernia, right?"

"Yeah," answered Billy.

"Okay, it's nine p.m., and all the doctors' offices are closed. Let me make some calls tomorrow morning, right after the offices open up. Then I'll call you and go over the plan with you, okay?" asked Warren.

"I guess so," replied Billy.

Warren turned to Maryann, who had a quizzical look on her face, and said, "Okay, Maryann, I'll see you tomorrow morning. Good night."

"But I have questions, and what's going on with Billy?" Maryann asked.

Warren smiled and, as he got into his Escalade, said, "I'll explain everything tomorrow morning."

The next morning at the diner, after eating breakfast and reviewing the split of the income, Warren gave Maryann a brief summary of Billy's health condition.

"Wow, Warren, it's great that you're helping Billy out with that. I feel better knowing that you've got his back. So now will you please explain what happened last night with Diaz?" Maryann asked.

Warren took a deep breath and answered, "The cartel has started to run their business the way other corporate giants do, like Walmart. They realized that infighting would only allow a rival operation to step in and begin to take market share. Currently, Diaz's cartel owns the northeast, and they want to keep it that way."

"How does that help us and keep MS-13 out of our business?" asked Maryann.

"Simple, but hold that thought." Warren picked up his cell phone and called Steven. "Hey, can you make a phone call to Island Surgical in Bay Shore for Billy? Yeah, he needs that surgery as soon as possible. Thanks. Bye."

Steven replied, "Consider it done, but I'll text you with the info when everything's confirmed."

Warren turned back to Maryann, paused as if to remember what they had been talking about, and said, "Every time there was infighting among gangs in the same organization, that gang lost market share because the clients didn't want to get caught in the crossfire. And they, the clients, started buying their drugs from a totally new gang. Diaz's cartel *used to* control the Texas border market. They got a piece of everything that came over, but their gangs started infighting, and long story short, Diaz's cartel no longer controls the border. The cartel doesn't want that to happen here. The cartel is making us a deal because we deliver a higher profit and the lowest amount of problems. They're no different from Google or Amazon—they want to own 100 percent of the market. That way, no competitor will challenge them because the cost of acquiring new clients will be too high. Does that agreement mean that we will be safe forever? Absolutely *not*. We probably have five years before all this blows up in our faces.

"Maryann," Warren paused and took a deep breath again and said, "honestly, Steven and I plan to leave in three to six months for parts unknown. When we leave, the business is yours."

Maryann's face gave away her feelings of anxiety, and she said, "I'm not sure I want all this and the headache with Diaz and MS-13." Just then, Warren's cell phone rang with a text message from Steven: "Billy situation all done."

Warren stopped reading and continued, "Come on, we have discussed this. I told you eventually we would be leaving. Don't give me that look. Let me finish." Maryann nodded her head, and Warren continued, "And I'm going to want you to purchase and move into my house. It has all the protection you need. The apartment complex can never be as secure as my place. If you're interested in all the other business entities I own, I would like to sell them to you for two reasons. First, I know you have the cash." They both laughed. "And secondly, you need more legit business income so when you are ready, you can sell the drug franchise back to the cartel or Diaz and get out. Even if you can't sell the franchise, you need enough legit income to live off of, and then you will get out because you are smart enough to realize that this train is short-lived. And if you stay in too long, it is a matter of *when*, not *if*, you're going to jail. I know neither of us planned to be in this business, but it was a way out of the mess we were in, correct?" Warren looked at Maryann for an answer. She nodded yes.

"What do you want?" Warren asked.

"Enough money to support what I want to do and live. Never end up living in my car," answered Maryann emotionally.

"Well, that lifestyle has a cost to it. And honestly, you don't have any cash to support any lifestyle yet," answered Warren.

Maryann nodded, knowing his assessment of her financial situation was correct. She didn't have enough cash, and for that moment, she flashed back to when she was living in her car and Davie opened her broken car door. She felt a tremble go through her body. She knew then she wanted enough money to provide her with that security and a lifestyle that she didn't have to depend on anyone else or do anything she didn't want to do and live in a place of comfort.

"Maryann," Warren continued, "I think you are going to want to do what Steve and I are doing, which is disappearing with the cash and starting a new life without the worry of guys like Diaz and MS-13 around."

Maryann looked up and said "yes, exactly" empathically.

"Okay," said Warren. "It will take you a couple years, maybe three years, to amass that amount of money if you take over all my businesses so you can disappear."

Warren looked at his watch and then looked back at Maryann and said, "It's getting late. You have deliveries to make and a 7-Eleven business you must check on, and I have a bunch of stuff that has to get done. I will give you a call around nine to answer any of your questions."

Maryann nodded and said, "Okay." But in her mind, she knew Warren's businesses offered the only solution to her getting out.

At nine o'clock, Warren called Maryann, "Hi, just following up. Any questions or concerns?" asked Warren.

"I can't talk right now," Maryann answered.

"Is there a problem?" Warren asked in an anxious tone.

"No," replied Maryann with a little bit of an attitude. "Just learning 7-Eleven procedures. I understand what and the why of what you are doing. I just need to wrap my head around all this and figure out if this is good for me. If I have any questions, I will call you later."

"Okay, bye." As Warren pushed the button to end the call, he started wondering if the deal with Maryann would go through. The more he thought about the conversation with Maryann, the more concerned he became.

As if on cue, Warren's cell phone rang; it was Billy. "Hey, Billy, go to 15 Park Avenue in Bay Shore to Island Surgical. Go to the front desk and give them your name. They are expecting you. And if the operation needs to be done ASAP, they will do the pre-op testing and get you admitted to Good Sam."

"Thanks, Warren. I really appreciate it," Billy said.

"No problem. Get well and call me when you get back home," Warren said.

Later that day, Warren and Steven agreed to purchase the property in Northern Idaho. Warren instructed Steven to call Black Ops and ask when they could start the improvements to the property and, more importantly, how long it would take to complete all the upgrades.

"Steven," Warren stated, "my concern is I want to be out of here in three months. I feel we are living on borrowed time. The OD epidemic is getting very hot. The local police and feds, because of MS-13, are all over Long Island looking for drug dealers who have caused these ODs. At most, we have three months, so we need to have all the improvements done by then. Is this possible?"

"I will call Black Ops and tell them what you need and the time frame. I assume you would prefer it all done in thirty days?" asked Steven.

"Yes, that would be perfect. Also ask how much this will all cost."

Steven got on the phone with Black Ops right away to get the process started. He also requested them to get a sign for the entrance, which would read "Eagle's Nest."

The next day, Steven got a call from Black Ops to inspect the four caves and determine which ones are best for the tunnels and the underground bunker installed; the extra security would be an additional $275,000.

"Warren, the one thing they need to know is the number of people in the bunker so they can buy enough supplies and make it the right size," Steven reported.

"Ten," Warren shouted back. Then in a lower voice, Warren asked, "Should we get two, with each able to hold five?" He walked out of the safe room and into the kitchen, where Steven was.

They were both standing by the kitchen island when Steven replied, "No. If there is a breakdown of civil society and government, we are going to need one another to survive. The real problem with having two bunkers is a mindset of us versus them could set in, and infighting would start. Warren, you have to remember that this bunker will be stored in the mine caves connected to the homes with escape tunnels. Once the bunker is activated, the tunnel doors are locked and sealed. The outside openings to the caves will be sealed once the bunker is completed, so the ten people aren't being stuck in the bunker. They will have the entire mine caves to roam through."

"Okay, solid argument. One bunker for ten," Warren answered.

"I assume that eight of the ten slots are for your six platoon buddies and us, but who are the other two slots for?" Steven asked.

Warren smiled and shrugged his shoulders. "I don't know," he told Steven, but after a pause, Warren looked at Steven and said, "You should make the number fifteen."

"Fifteen?" Steven said in a surprised voice. "I bet one of those spots is for Maryann."

Warren replied quickly and defensively, "Absolutely *not*. That would jeopardize our entire security and the reason we are doing all this. The slots are for good friends and people who are important to us."

After a long silent pause, Steven stated, "That settles it. Maryann is getting one of those slots. And by the way, how are we getting all our stuff to Eagle's Nest?"

"Call Hopscotch Air at Republic and ask to speak with the owner, Doug. Tell him the size we need, and they will get the plane and pilot for the trip. But I think Maryann is going to want all the furniture and stuff. We are going to bring our clothes, movies, CDs, books, computers, printers, important papers, and cash."

"Don't forget your paintings," Steven said.

"The paintings? No. I think Maryann will want them. I'll take the painting equipment but leave the paintings."

"You *hope* she wants them," Steven replied with a grin.

"Why wouldn't she want them?" asked Warren. "They are paintings of the Great South Bay, sunsets, boats, and sandy beaches."

"Maybe they're not her style or taste," replied Steven.

"Good point," Warren replied. "Well, tomorrow I'm going to bring Maryann back to the house so she can look around and to get her to commit to purchasing it. I'll see if she wants the paintings then."

Steven asked, "When is she coming, and are we serving dinner?"

"Around seven o'clock," Warren replied. "And yes on the dinner." Warren continued, "Hey, we forgot about the wine cellar. Pick a wine for tonight and tomorrow's dinner and pack the rest of the wine cellar for Eagle's Nest."

"Okay, got it," Steven replied.

At the four o'clock breakfast meeting the next morning, Warren seemed distracted. He admitted that he was preoccupied with the move to Eagle's Nest and the situation with Diaz. So Maryann suggested they cut the meeting short and just discuss essentials. Then Warren went back home to help Steven with the move preparations.

Steven and Warren didn't talk much throughout the day; both were busy sorting and packing in separate rooms. When they finally took a break in the afternoon, Steven said, "I picked out a nice Chianti for dinner tonight. Do you think Maryann will like that?"

"Oh shit! I completely forgot to invite her over at the meeting this morning. I better call her right now."

As Warren picked up the phone to call Maryann, Steven just shook his head and rolled his eyes at Warren; he had made it sound like it was already a done deal that she was coming over.

"Hey, Maryann, this is Warren."

"I know. I have you in my caller ID. What's up? Got more problems with Diaz?"

"No, no," answered Warren. The tone of his voice showed he understood the fear that Maryann had for Diaz. "The reason I'm calling is to ask you to come to my house for dinner so you can do a walk-through and see if you want to buy it."

"When?" asked Maryann.

"Tonight around seven," answered Warren.

"You're not giving me much notice," Maryann stated.

"I apologize. With all the stuff we are doing for the move, it wasn't until late last night that I realized I hadn't had you over for a walk-through of the house. I didn't want to call you late last night, and it slipped my mind this morning. So can you make it?" asked Warren.

"Sure," Maryann replied.

"Great," replied Warren. "Then I'll see you at seven."

CHAPTER 11

Right at seven that evening, the doorbell rang. "Who could it be?" Steven asked, teasing Warren.

Warren rolled his eyes and shook his head at Steven as if to say, "Grow up." He didn't want Steven to know that he was actually nervous. "Good evening, Maryann. Come in. Your dress is beautiful," Warren said as he opened the door.

"Oh, thank you," Maryann responded as she entered the house.

"You already know my brother, Steven," Warren said.

"Of course, I met him the other night, but we haven't been formally introduced," Maryann answered.

"Well, there are absolutely no formalities here," Steven responded, laughing as the three of them stood in the foyer. Steven had a kitchen towel over his shoulder and was drying his hands, then he asked, "What would you like to do first, eat or see the house?"

"Let's eat. I'm starving," Maryann replied.

"You got it," Steven replied. "We are having our father's favorite: spaghetti with meatballs and sausages. And, of course, garlic bread and a red wine that was specially chosen by yours truly for this occasion."

Warren poured the wine and gave a toast: "To good health, to successful business ventures, and may you be able to ride off into the sunset of life on your own terms." All three laughed, sipped the wine, and started eating.

While eating, Maryann started asking about the house, "When was the house built?"

Steven replied because Warren's mouth was full of spaghetti, "The house was completely rebuilt after Hurricane Sandy. In the reconstruction, we added specific security measures that were recommended by Black Ops. The entire perimeter of the house, the grounds, and the inside of the house are monitored by cameras with facial recognition and thermal imaging. If something occurs, we get messages sent to our phones. One of the great things about the thermal imaging was seeing heat loss. I guess the builder didn't put enough insulation in the walls because in the corner and around the windows, it was all blue. So we hired a contractor to blow insulation into the walls where the gaps were to reduce energy loss."

At the end of the main course, Steven asked Maryann if she wanted to take the tour of the house next and have dessert after or have dessert and take the tour later. Maryann immediately replied, "Let's take the tour first and have dessert later. I need a little time to digest." Then Maryann asked, "Do you guys always eat like this?"

Steven and Warren just nodded their heads. Then Steven said, "Why do you think there is a full exercise room in this house? It's to work off the food we love but doesn't leave us until we sweat it off."

Maryann smiled back and said, "Every woman knows that story."

Steven gave the tour while Warren cleaned off the table. "We wanted it to be open so as you walk in, your eyes go right to the back wall of windows and glass doors and you see the Great South Bay. As you can see, the dining room, kitchen, and family room are all one big space separated by the high bar. By the way, the fireplace runs on gas, but it can also work with wood logs, and it throws off a lot of heat, enough to warm this entire room in the winter months."

Maryann said, "I see you have a big-screen TV there."

"Yeah," replied Steven. "We like to sit there and relax at the end of the day. That's why the chairs had to be very comfortable." Steve continued, "Behind the fireplace wall is the master bedroom, full bathroom, and another bedroom or study."

As they walked through the doorway into the hallway of the master bedroom, Maryann spotted a picture of someone she recognized. "That's Billy," she said, smiling as she was speaking. "He's a really nice guy. How did his operation go?"

"It went well," Steven replied. "We might see him tonight. He said he might stop by." He stopped in the hallway to show the bedroom and said, "Warren uses this one as an office."

"What's with the full-size mirror in the office?" Maryann asked.

Steve replied, "Warren is sometimes a little vain and wants to make sure everything looks just right. You know, like every hair in the right place." They both laughed. They walked farther down the hallway to the master bath. As they walked into the master bedroom, Maryann stopped and looked at the view. "Wow," she said. "The view of the bay is magnificent."

"Let's go upstairs," Steven said.

As they got to the top step, Maryann just said, "Wow!"

Steven said, "Yeah, we wanted all the toys you could imagine. This is the game room. Off to the left is the theater, with the biggest screen they made at the time, and six of the most comfortable chairs. Next to the theater is the library."

As they crossed the game room, Maryann commented, "I like the French doors."

Steven went on to show Maryann the exercise room and more magnificent views of the bay. Then he motioned her to follow him through a door that looked like the others, but Maryann detected it didn't lead to an ordinary room. As they stepped into a dark room with several flat-screen TVs on the wall, Steven closed the door behind them and turned to Maryann and told her, "This is the safe room." He pointed out another bathroom and a closet with shelves filled with MREs (meals ready to eat) and a console with a lot of buttons. "In here you have enough food and water to survive a month, communication equipment to connect with the outside world, and a bathroom. But more importantly, this console is the brains of the security of the house. There are two consoles in the house. One is downstairs in Warren's study, but the one in the study is deactivated once the safe room console is activated. I was here when Juan's people surrounded the house." Steven flipped a switch, and all the TV screens went on. Steven continued, "From here, you can see every room and square inch of the property."

"What's that moving? Are the cameras infrared?" asked Maryann.

"Oh, that's the neighbor's cat. I have yet to figure out where it is going and why it keeps coming onto our property," Steven replied. "Two of the switches I want to show you are this one marked shades—

those are armored metal shades that come down over all the windows and doors to protect us from intruders or another Hurricane Sandy, and yes, the shades are bulletproof—and this one marked sniper's revenge. On the roof of the house, the garage, and the underside of the bridge that leads to the garage, there are guns that can target individuals on the property. And with this button under the switch, you can fire bullets at an individual or group of individuals and take them down before they realize what is going on. When Juan was starting to surround the house, I flipped this switch. The shades came down, and this switch activated the guns, but they backed away before I needed to take any action, which was good."

Steven motioned to Maryann to open the door to leave, and then he continued, "There is another large storage room on the other side of the kitchen. We call it the vault. Do you want to see it?"

"No," said Maryann. "I can imagine what it is used for with that name." They both laughed.

As they walked downstairs, Steven told her, "Over the garage is another huge bonus room. At least that's what the builder called it."

"Let me guess," Maryann said, "another vault?"

"Yes, but we also store Christmas decorations there." Steven motioned to the left and said, "Here is another bathroom, which is for guests, and over here are two pantries and a mudroom. Across from it is the laundry room, and this door takes you into the garage, where there is a staircase to the bonus room."

"Okay, guys, it's time for dessert!" Warren yelled out.

As Steven and Maryann walked backed to the dining room, Maryann asked Steven, "Who painted all these landscapes and seascapes? They're good. I can actually picture myself in the painting."

Steven replied, "Only one painter, and you get only one guess."

"You!" Maryann answered excitedly.

"No, no, they are Warren's. It's his way of escaping or coping with the horrors of war and people letting him down. I think he escapes into every painting he paints. Take that one over there with the two palm trees with the hammock and the sun setting. The two trees signify two people. The hammock is what holds them together, but the darkness of the colors and the setting sun mean their relationship is over. He painted that when his wife died."

"Finally," Warren said, "you guys are back." Warren looked at Maryann and asked, "Regular coffee? Demitasse? Tea?"

"Demitasse," Maryann replied.

"Would you like sugar with that?" Warren asked. "And I would just like to point out the dessert options on the Viennese table: Oreo cookies, the special black-and-white cookies, and my favorite—the Italian rainbow cookie cake. Dig in."

The three of them reached for the Italian rainbow cookie cake. After Maryann tasted one, she said, "This is good. Where did you get it?"

"The bakery at Best Market by you," Warren responded.

After they finished the demitasse and dessert, the conversation turned to business.

"Okay," started Warren, "you've seen the house and all the specialty items we have installed for our protection, which would be for your protection also. Do we have a deal?"

"The 1 million includes furniture and paintings?" Maryann asked.

"Which paintings?" Warren asked.

"All of them," Maryann responded.

"I'm not sure. Some of the paintings, I'm attached to," Warren said, slowly emphasizing the words *attached to.*

Maryann started to negotiate. "Can this attachment be broken? After all, it is an unknown artist because he, or she, never signed the work."

Warren smiled and said, "Possibly."

"Okay," Maryann said, "there are twelve of them. I will give you an additional 100,000."

Warren just shook his head no and said, "They mean more to me than $8,333 per painting."

Maryann said, "Well, they aren't worth 12,000."

Warren responded quickly, "No, but they are worth 10,000!"

Maryann smiled and said, "Sold! $120,000."

"Good, I have given you a list of all the other properties and businesses I own and want to sell," Warren continued. "Do you have any questions?"

Maryann said, "I saw you own two 7-Eleven stores and five apartment complexes, one of which is the one I live in, and you want 21 million for it all. Based on my cash flow, I'll pay 18 million—10 million in cash and the rest in monthly payments."

Warren replied, "15 million in all cash, no payments."

"Agreed," answered Maryann.

"So to recap," Warren began, "$15 million for the businesses and 1.12 million for the house and paintings in cash."

"Correct," Maryann replied and then asked, "When do you want to close?"

"On the businesses," Warren answered, "as soon as possible. The house, three to six months, maybe sooner."

CHAPTER 12

The next morning, Warren called Hopscotch Air. "Good morning, this is Warren. Is Doug in?"

"Yes, what is this in reference to?" the operator asked.

"Booking a charter flight to Mexico."

"Okay, I'll put you through," the operator replied.

"Hey, Warren, good morning. We are working on getting that plane to Idaho for you. Is that why you're calling?" Doug asked.

"No," Warren replied. "I need to fly to Mexico, and I need a plane big enough to carry a 112-cubic-foot container that weighs 551 pounds as soon as you can."

"To go that distance, you are going to need a Learjet 35. Anyone going with you?" Doug asked.

"Probably just me, but I haven't got it all together yet," Warren replied.

So one definite and possibly another person and the cargo?" Doug asked.

"No, it's just going to be me and the cargo," replied Warren.

"Okay, let me scout out the available Learjets and available pilots. I assume you want this done on the QT?" Doug asked.

"Correct," Warren replied.

A few days later, Doug called Warren.

"Hello, Doug, have you found a plane and pilot for me?" asked Warren.

"Yes, Warren, and it can be here in two days, Thursday morning," Doug replied. "When did you think you'll have the freight ready to ship? If you need freight boxes, we have them. I think you are going to need at least one based on what you told me."

"Okay, can you send one to the house on South Merrick Road that you have on file?"

"Sure. I'll have it delivered this afternoon," Doug responded.

"Great! I will see you Thursday, around noon, for a trip to Mexico City." After Warren got off the phone with Doug, he called Diaz.

"Good morning, Diaz, this is Warren. I need the name and number of the art dealer we discussed."

"Hey, Warren, sure. The owner's name is Raúl Diaz, Mexico City Art Auctions. Number is 52-55-5514-9788. The outside of the building looks like a house—white stucco and a brown-stained wood front door. The front of the building has large glass windows. The gallery is inside, and the auction room is upstairs."

"Is this guy a relative of yours?" Warren asked.

"Yes," Diaz said with a laugh, "a distant cousin. But based on our conversations, I told Raúl to expect you, and he has two guys who will bid on your painting up to $50 million. The auction will start at two thirty p.m. Yours will be one of three paintings to be auctioned off."

"What's the security like?" Warren asked.

"Warren, don't worry. They do great work there. Security is up to the job, and no one will mess with you," Diaz answered.

Thursday morning came quickly. Warren was at the safe house ready to meet the truck driver when he knocked on the front door. Warren opened the door, and the truck driver said "Good morning, Warren" as he looked at the clipboard. "I'm here to pick up one cargo container for today's flight to—" He looked back to the clipboard and read, "Mexico City."

"It's in the first garage stall," Warren said. "Let me open the door for you." As Warren pressed the button to raise the door, the morning sunlight exposed the cargo container. The truck driver attached the container to the truck and began to lift it onto the vehicle. Once the cargo container was on the truck, the driver had Warren sign for it.

"See you later at the airport," the driver said. Warren smiled and waved goodbye.

As the truck left, Warren thought, *There goes 50 million. I hope nothing happens.* He continued watching the truck until it was out of sight, then he walked back into the house and called Steven to tell him that the container just left for the airport and that he would be home soon to get his things and head to the airport. "The plane leaves at nine, so we'll be in Mexico City by one p.m."

Steven asked, "Are you sure you don't want me to come along?"

"No," Warren quickly answered. "There's a lot that needs to be done so we can move on time. I need you here to accomplish those things."

"Okay," Steven replied. "Just making sure."

Warren drove home and picked up his backpack and the boxed painting. He said goodbye to Steven and drove off. He arrived at Republic Airport and parked in the Hopscotch Air hangar. When he spotted Doug and the Learjet, he called out, "Hey, Doug, is my cargo container on board?"

"Yes," Doug replied, "and the pilot is waiting to leave." Doug led Warren to the cabin door. Warren walked inside and waved goodbye to Doug as the attendant closed the door.

The cabin was luxurious, with a white leather chair and an executive desk on one side; on the other side was a long white couch. Warren walked to the executive desk and placed the painting on the floor next to it. In what felt like minutes, the plane had taken off and was heading toward Mexico City. The attendant walked up to Warren and asked if he wanted anything and told him the plane was fully stocked with food and beverage.

Warren replied, "I would like a cup of coffee and a roast beef sandwich."

"I will serve you as soon as we reach cruising altitude," the attendant replied.

Warren smiled and said, "Thank you."

The five-hour flight seemed to go fast, and in no time, the pilot called out and said they were landing in Mexico City. "We will touch down in ten minutes," he said. As they were taxiing to the hangar, Warren got a call from Doug.

"Hey, Doug, what's up?"

"Warren, the plane will go right into the hangar. Once the plane comes to a stop, the cargo container will be removed and placed on a truck to deliver it to the Raúl Diaz Gallery. The truck has space for you. So wait until the container is on the truck. Once that is done, the cargo people will come to get you."

Ten minutes later, the truck was in front of the art gallery. After pulling around to the freight entrance, Warren watched as the cargo container was transferred from the truck into the building. Satisfied that his precious cargo had made it safely to its destination, he went inside and asked where he could find Raúl.

One of the workers said, "You will find Señor Diaz on the auction floor upstairs. He is expecting you, Señor Warren."

"Could you please show me the way?" Warren replied.

"Yes, sure," the worker replied. As Warren and the worker reached upstairs, he walked over to a gentleman and said, "Señor Diaz, Señor Warren is here."

As they were shaking hands, Señor Diaz asked Warren, "Do you have the painting?"

"Yes, it's right here," Warren replied and handed it over to Señor Diaz.

"Please call me Raúl. Señor Diaz is my father. Nice frame. Makes it look even more valuable," Raúl said then gestured toward another room and said, "Follow me." As the two men walked through a doorway, he said, "This is the auction room." It was a large room with white walls and rows of chairs divided by an aisle in the middle—about twenty-five chairs on either side. In front of the room was a large movable white wall, where the painting to be auctioned off was to be hung; there was a painting of a blue sky already hung on it.

Raúl pointed to the white wall and said, "Your painting will be hung here during the auction."

"Okay, but how is this going to be done?" Warren asked.

Raúl explained, "Two of my men will start the bid at $1 million. One will be in the room, and the other will be online. They will go back and forth until they reach 50 million."

"Are they going to be the only two at the auction?" asked Warren.

"No. Didn't my cousin explain this to you?" Raúl asked.

"Yes," Warren replied, "but I just want to make sure."

"Okay," Raúl continued, "your painting will be one of three. The other two are considered Mexico's greatest masterpieces. One painting is of landscapes, and the other is of a building in Mexico City. That blue-sky painting on the wall is one of them. We are hoping that goes for 100 million. The artist's last painting sold for 75 million. Regarding your painting, we have placed the money you brought down in a house account. Once the bidding is complete, we will transfer that money into the auction house account. All buyers' money is placed into this account once the payment has been settled. In your case, the funds will be available immediately, which means we will wire transfer the money into your New York bank account minus our fee. My fee, I'm sure my cousin told you, is 10 percent."

Warren nodded his head.

"So at the end of the day, 45 million will be deposited into your account. Does that all make sense, Warren?

"Yes," Warren responded.

"Oh, by the way, yours is the last painting, and the auction will be starting in a few minutes," Raúl stated then smiled and walked away.

The auctioneer took the stage and began the bidding at 25 million. Quickly, the bids ran up to 75 million. By now, spectators and serious bidders filled the room. A man with a beard wearing a golf hat raised the bid to $75,500,000. His card had number 26. Just then, a person sitting at the computer raised her hand and said, "80 million." A third person dressed in a suit, like he just stepped out of a *GQ* ad, raised his card number 69 to raise the bid to 81 million.

The golf-hat guy, who was otherwise well-dressed, turned ever so slightly to see who had just raised the bid. He then turned back to the auctioneer, raised his card, and stated, "82 million." The internet bidder then increased the bid to 83 million.

The well-dressed *GQ* guy was sitting next to an equally well-dressed and beautiful lady wearing expensive jewelry. She nudged him. He raised his card ever so slightly. The auctioneer stated, "Number 69 raises the bid to 84 million?" It was asked more like a question, to be sure the gentleman was really bidding that amount. The gentleman nodded. At that point, the woman dealing with the internet bidder shot her arm up. The auctioneer acknowledged her, and she stated with a faint smile, "88 million."

Warren was watching all this and thinking, *These three people either really want this painting or don't want the others to have it.* Mr. GQ raised his card again, and the auctioneer stated, "89 million."

The internet bidder raised it to 90 million, and then the golfer raised his card and said, rather loudly, "100 million."

When no one raised their card to counter his bid, the auctioneer said, "100 million once, 100 million twice, sold to card number 26." Once the auctioneer banged his gavel for the third time, the golfer turned slightly to smile at Mr. GQ. Warren watched all this and detected a rivalry between the two men; the golfer's smile was more like a jab.

Warren watched as the next painting was being hung on the wall. The painting was of a Mexico City neighborhood corner building that was three stories tall. The first floor was all stores and a restaurant. The picture reminded Warren of a building in Sorrento, Italy. There was a warmth about the picture. Maybe it was the smiles on the faces of the people in the picture. They looked like they were enjoying themselves.

The auctioneer started the bidding at 25 million, and an internet bidder entered the next bid at 26 million. The golf man and the *GQ* gentleman were still in the audience. The *GQ* gentleman was the first to raise his card to 27 million, and the golf man quickly raised it to 28. Immediately, the *GQ* man raised his card, and the auctioneer said, "29 million." Warren thought, *Here we go again.*

For this auction, there were two internet operators and two phone operators monitoring the bidding. One of the internet monitors raised her arm and said, "31 million." The second internet monitor raised his arm for 35, and a phone bidder increased it to 40 million.

At this point, the golf man jumped in and raised his card and said, "43 million." Mr. GQ smiled and quickly topped his bid to 45 million. Warren thought that bid seemed like a jab back at the golfer. Then an internet operator raised her arm and stated, "48," and a few seconds later, the other internet operator raised his arm and said, "50." The golfer raised his card and said, "53." The *GQ* man stated, "54 million," and the golfer quickly replied, "56." His smile was another jab at the *GQ* gentleman.

The auctioneer started his count, "56 million going once, twice, and three times."

Warren began thinking about how the sale of his painting was his chance to launder his drug money into legal tender. As he looked up, his painting was being hung. He thought to himself, *As soon as this is over, I want to get back to the States.*

The auctioneer started to describe the painting: "Two palm trees with one hammock tied between them. It would be a beautiful beach scene, but it is painted all in blue, signifying that the romance is over and the sun is setting on the relationship. The palm trees represent the individuals in the relationship, and they are tried together by the hammock. Even though the sun is dark, in the corner, you see a small shiny yellow light, which represents the eternal hope that their love can be rekindled and last forever."

Then the auctioneer stated, "We are going to start the bidding at $1 million."

One of the telephone operators raised his arm and said, "6," and immediately a guy from the floor raised his card number 2 and said, "8." Warren thought they must be the guys whom Raúl had mentioned, and things were going smoothly.

Just then, the telephone monitor raised his arm and said, "10," and the guy with card number 2 countered with 12. The telephone monitor raised his arm again and said, "15." At this point, the *GQ* gentleman started to take a closer look at the painting, and his lady friend was nudging him to bid on the artwork.

He raised his card and said, "20 million." Warren moved right behind the two bidders to try to hear what they were saying and to figure out if Mr. GQ was another of Raúl's plants to get the bidding process over. Warren got nervous when he overheard the lady say, "I must have this painting because it is about everlasting love."

Warren thought to himself, *No, lady, this painting is about a money transfer from illegal to legal money.*

Then the going-smoothly thought evaporated as the golf guy raised his card and stated, "I raise your bid to 23 million."

The telephone monitor stood and said, "We have 28 million." Raúl's guy in the room chimed in with 30. The telephone monitor raised his arm and told the auctioneer he had 31 million.

"Going once—"

The auctioneer started to raise his gavel when Raúl's guy with card number 2 raised it and said, "35 million."

The telephone monitor stated, "We have a bid for 40."

Just then, Mr. GQ got a nudge in the ribs by his lady friend, so he raised his card and said, "45."

Not to be outdone, the golfer guy raised his card and said, "50."

Warren thought, *Oh shit, the wrong guy bid 50!* The auctioneer looked to the telephone monitor to see if there was a higher bid. He shook his head. The auctioneer looked to Raúl's guy, who also shook his head. Warren looked directly at him, and he could see he didn't know what to do. He knew his bidding was only authorized to 50 million; he looked back at Warren and shrugged his shoulders.

Just then, Mr. GQ said, "60 million."

The auctioneer quickly said, "We have $60 million for this painting going once, 60 million twice, sold to cardholder number 69." The auctioneer continued, "Thank you all for participating in today's auction. Our next auction will be next Monday at noon. Thank you again and good day."

Mr. GQ's lady friend gave him a big kiss and quickly walked to the painting to examine it more closely. Warren sat stunned, not believing what had just happened.

CHAPTER 13

Raúl walked over to Warren and said, "Congratulations, Warren, your painting went for 10 million more than you needed." But the reaction Raúl got wasn't what he expected.

"I don't give a damn," Warren replied.

"What is the problem?" Raúl asked.

"You promised me this was a no-brainer," Warren started.

"Yeah, but you made $10 million more," Raúl replied sharply, still confused as to why Warren was so unhappy with the outcome.

"You don't understand," Warren replied. "That painting was part of a sale of my home. The buyer wanted the painting, and the price we agreed on includes it. Now what am I going to do? How are you going to clean my original 50 million that you have in your account? I am not pleased."

Raúl replied, "It looks like you have two options. One, go home now and consider the 54 million you got for your painting as the conversion of your money and paint a replica for the new owner. Or two, go to my house in Puerto Aventuras and paint *two* more paintings—a new one for next Monday's auction, where there will be only two buyers, and a replica for the new owner of your house."

"I guess I will take option two. I hope I have a second painting in me," Warren said.

"Good," Raúl replied. "I'll make arrangements with my villa manager, Sofia, to get you any supplies you need and to handle your stay at the villa. And by the way, thank you for my $6-million fee. It is a pleasure doing business with you."

"I assume this stay will be gratis?" Warren asked.

"Of course," Raúl answered. "You just made me $6 million. That is the least I could do. Tonight, I'll have my driver take you to the airport so you can board my plane to fly to Puerto Aventuras, and then Sofia will meet you at the airport and drive you to my villa. But before you leave, I need a list of the things you need to create the paintings."

"You will have it," answered Warren.

As Warren was leaving the gallery, he handed Raúl the list of supplies he needed for his painting.

Raúl replied, "Thank you. I will call Sofia now so she can get your supplies while you are in the air. Good luck painting."

"Thank you," Warren answered as he was entering the limo that would take him to the airport. On the way, Warren asked the driver how long it would it take to drive to Puerto Aventuras.

"It would be over nineteen hours," the driver answered. "But you wouldn't want to do that even if it were less because the illegals are walking to America's border and are using the same roads. It is not safe. But don't worry. The community where Raúl lives is a very secure neighborhood, with walls and armed guards. Mr. Raúl's neighbors demanded that. Last summer, Raúl let my family and me stay at his house. We felt the neighborhood was very impressive—very secure—and it is pretty much self-sufficient. Raúl and his partners hired a company called Black Ops to design the layout of the development to develop the security and everything to make the community fully self-sufficient."

As soon as the driver mentioned Black Ops, Warren leaned forward to catch every word. Warren asked, "Are all the lots sold?"

"No," said the driver. "Are you interested?"

"Yes, possibly," answered Warren.

"Sofia will be able to put you in touch with the Black Ops company people," replied the driver. By then, they had reached the airport and Raúl's plane. The driver came to a complete stop and pointed to a jet plane and said, "That is Raúl's plane. You will be in Puerto Aventuras in an hour, and Raúl just texted me to tell you Sofia has received your list of supplies." Warren thanked him for his assistance and climbed into the plane. Once in the aircraft, he was met by a pilot, copilot, and flight attendant.

As Warren sat down, the flight attendant introduced herself, "Hi, I'm Phyllis. Warren, right?"

"Yes," Warren replied. "Nice to meet you, Phyllis."

Just then, the copilot, José, introduced himself and said, "We do this flight a lot for Raúl, and the trip looks like it will be a smooth flight—no problems from the weather."

As José finished, the pilot came back and introduced himself, "Hi, I'm Chuck. The preflight checklist is complete. We are ready to take off whenever you are ready."

Warren replied, "Let's go."

Chuck turned to Phyllis and said, "Close the cabin door and secure all items."

Phyllis turned to Warren and said, "As soon as we are in the air, I'll stop by to see if you want anything to eat or drink."

"That will be fine," Warren replied.

As soon as Phyllis closed the cabin door, the plane started to move toward the runway; and in no time, they were in the air. As soon as the plane reached cruising altitude, Phyllis, as promised, came over and sat across from Warren and asked what he would like to drink and eat.

Warren replied, "Do you have a Coke and a sandwich?"

"Yes, we have a roast beef hero."

"That will be fine," Warren replied with a smile.

Phyllis brought Warren his food and asked if she could join him. "Yes, please," Warren replied. "I don't like eating alone. That would be great."

Phyllis got a cup of coffee and sat across from Warren.

Warren started the conversation by asking where they would be landing.

Phyllis replied, "We will be landing at the private airport inside the neighborhood. It is just for the residents of the community. One of the men from Black Ops told me that they wanted the community to be as secure as your White House but have all the amenities of the most luxurious resort in the world and be self-sustainable. I think the Black Ops guy said if the world descended into chaos, the standard of living would continue without interruption. That was one of the reasons why my husband and I purchased a small place there."

Warren replied with a smile. He started to think about Eagle's Nest and how happy he was with the contract with Black Ops for his new home in Idaho. Clearly, they understand what their clients want and need. He also began to think about purchasing a place in Puerto Aventuras for a place to escape the frigid winters in Idaho.

Just then, Chuck, the pilot, announced, "Buckle up. We will be landing shortly." Then as the plane was taxiing to the hangar, he said, "As you get off the aircraft, don't be surprised to see individuals with guns greeting you. They are the Black Ops security team."

As the plane came to a stop inside the hangar, Chuck came back to explain the disembarkation procedure. "Okay, Warren, this is how they handle security here: the crew leaves first with the flight paperwork, then the passengers file out one by one." Chuck went on to say, "I know Raúl called ahead to let the security team know you're coming, so there shouldn't be any delay, and Sofia will be here to drive you to Raúl's home."

Phyllis, Chuck, and José left the plane, and once they were down the stairs, Warren started down. The guard at the bottom of the stairs raised his hand and motioned for Warren to stop. After a few minutes, the guard motioned for Warren to continue down the stairs. As Warren reached the ground, he could see an officer was talking with the crew and smiling, and it looked like he was joking around with them. Phyllis turned and said, "Goodbye, Warren. Hope you have an enjoyable stay. Sofia will call us when you are ready to return to Mexico City."

Warren smiled and said, "Thank you," then he turned to the officer and was about to introduce himself. The officer raised his hand and said, "No introductions are needed here, Warren. We are well-aware of who you are and the purpose of your visit. I want to personally thank you for your past business with Black Ops. Our business success depends on your satisfaction each and every time you engage us. Thank you for that confidence."

Standing behind the officer was a tall pretty dark-haired young lady. The officer turned to introduce her. "Warren, this is Sofia, Raúl's property manager. If you have any questions, she will be able to answer them for you. I hope you have a restful stay. Good night."

Sofia asked, "Do you have any luggage?"

"No," Warren answered, "just my backpack." The conversation continued as Warren got into the car.

"Good," replied Sofia. "Your supplies have arrived, and they are at the house. Do you have any questions?"

"Not now," Warren replied, "but tomorrow I would like a tour of the development."

"Anything special or specific you would like to see?"

Warren said, "Not sure. I really don't know anything about the development, but I'd like to get a sense of the community and the lay of the land, security, amenities, culture, etc. Basically what makes this place unique."

As Sofia opened the door to the house, she turned to Warren and said, "We can talk tomorrow. For now, the house has six bedrooms. I have put your supplies in the master bedroom, which is at the top of the stairs. The house has a pool and many other amenities, but we can go over that in the morning. Good night. We will talk in the morning about the tour."

The next morning, Warren was up early. He had gone downstairs, found his way to the kitchen to make coffee, and was sipping his coffee as he surveyed the property. As he walked outside, he saw a big pool, a hot tub, and a lagoon that flows into the ocean. Suddenly Warren heard Sofia saying, "Good morning. Do you want breakfast?"

"No, thanks," Warren replied. "I'm good with my coffee right now."

"Do you want to take a tour of the development now, or do you wish to begin your painting?" Before he could answer, his cell phone went off. It was Steven.

"Hey, Steven, what's up?" Warren asked.

"Remember that girl Caroline, Maryann's client?" Steven paused.

"No, not really. Why?" Warren answered.

"She's dead, likely OD. Maryann had been supplying her directly, and her boyfriend is asking questions all over, trying to find out who was supplying her."

"Okay, got it. Say no more. I will be home on Tuesday. Tell Maryann to lie low. No direct deals, get all new cell phones for the three of us, and call Black Ops. Make sure everything is going to be done by the end of the month. If possible, push them to see if it can be done sooner. If not, we may have to come down here first then go to Eagle's Nest. The Black Ops company runs this place."

Steven interrupted, "Where are you? I don't think Black Ops runs Mexico City."

"Oh, yes, I'm sorry. I'm in Puerto Aventuras, in Raúl Diaz's home. It's a long story that I will tell you later. Things got screwed up at the auction. Black Ops runs the community that Diaz owns a home in. They developed the complete community for the same reasons we are doing Eagle's Nest."

"Okay, understood. I will tell Maryann to get new phones. You will be back on Tuesday?" Steven asked.

"Yes, I will be back Tuesday. Text me the status of Eagle's Nest when you find out," Warren instructed.

"Okay," replied Steven.

"Sofia, I have to be back in New York no later than Tuesday morning. At lunch today, I would like to have a conversation with you about this community and what properties are ready to be moved into. Okay, I need to get started on the two paintings I have to do. Adios."

Sofia replied, "Hasta luego."

Warren went right to work on the paintings. He decided to paint the one to be auctioned off on Monday first. On a piece of paper, he wrote the title *Clouds over Mexico City*. After a while, the painting started to take shape. It was a landscape. In the bottom left of the canvas, he had painted some Aztec pyramids; on the right, a modern city; and in the middle, Mexico's highest mountain peak, Pico de Orizaba. Towering over the city and pyramids, the mountain appeared to pierce the clouds.

About noontime, Sofia walked into the master bedroom and said, "Hello, Warren. Are you ready for lunch?"

"Almost. I need to put the finishing touches on the cloud people," Warren answered.

"Cloud people?" Sofia asked.

"Yes," replied Warren. "The painting is called *Clouds over Mexico City*. Ever since I watched a National Geographic special on climbing Mount Kilimanjaro, I began noticing the clouds over cities. Italy has very few clouds, and the ones they have are flat, which I believe means no problem. Africa's clouds are big and rough in texture, meaning big problems ahead. And in Texas and Mexico, the clouds are like cotton balls, and you can see the shapes of people, animals, or other things in them."

"Does that have a meaning?" asked Sofia.

"Yes," Warren said. "In my mind, a lot of issues are facing both nations, but it appears that the cloud people, possibly our ancestors, will help us navigate those issues."

As Sofia studied the painting, she began to see the people Warren had painted.

"I see them!" she exclaimed. "There's a dog, a seated baby, a woman looking down at the baby, a soldier, and a shark."

Warren was wiping his hands clean when he said, "I'm glad that you see them. There are more, but it is time for lunch, and the painting needs to dry before I start the palm trees painting."

As they sat down at the kitchen table, Warren looked out the window and saw the beach, the pool, the outside grill, and the hot tub. *All very inviting*, he thought, *but I have to finish the palm tree painting before I can play. Maybe tomorrow.*

Sofia started to speak, when there was a knock on the door. Sofia turned to Warren and said, "I think our visitor will be able to answer all your questions regarding the community." When the visitor walked into the kitchen, Warren recognized him right away—the officer from the airport.

"Hi, Warren. My name is James. I am the property manager for Black Ops. Sofia tells me that you are interested in buying a property in our development."

"Yes," Warren said, "but I'm concerned about security."

"As you know, Black Ops specializes in security from all types of threats and the ability for our clients to continue their lifestyle regardless of what is happening outside the community. We have backup power and the ability to generate our own power, we grow our own crops, we even have our own aquaculture that produces a wide variety of fish, and you are aware of the security personnel that reside in the community."

"My concern," said Warren, "is not so much with the outside forces but with the inner forces."

James looked puzzled and said, "Everyone here has been chosen or, rather, *allowed* to buy into this community because of their skills. I'm not sure I understand your concerns."

"My concern," said Warren, "is the cartel. If we have a problem, is it allowed to spill into this community?"

"No, absolutely not," said James. By his tone, Warren could tell that he wouldn't put up with that type of behavior. "Listen, this is Switzerland. You leave the garbage outside. You are to behave respectfully inside the community."

Warren said, "To be sure I understand you, let me give you an example. One member of this community stops doing business with another member of this community. Outside these walls, that's punishable by death. What happens here?"

"Okay, I understand. Whoever starts the fight, he or she and their entire family will be expelled. Black Ops and the trustees of the community will buy back their membership and assets at a quick-sale price, collect their belongings, and ship it anywhere they want." James went on, "And then they can't come back, period. The theory is we need to make this place a safe haven, and unfortunately, we already had to expel someone. What we didn't anticipate were other people in the community interfering in the process of expelling the family, so the company and community as a whole agreed there would be one appeal process. Once decided, if you resist the decision, which is made by the elected community board members, the resisters and their families are expelled too. We don't want to happen here what happens in your country, where elected officials don't follow the laws and people don't abide by election results and think it is their right because they disagree with you. It isn't okay to get in your face. That won't happen here. Do you still want to buy a property here, understanding the rules by which you must live?"

Warren said, "Being civil and giving respect have never been a problem for me. Yes, I am still interested in properties that can be occupied immediately."

"Okay," James said, "we have two properties that can be occupied immediately, but I think only one will meet with your approval. It is called Casa Selva. It's in the heart of the jungle, fully self-sustainable with all the amenities. There is fresh water on the lot, and a few steps from the house are underground stalactite caves, where wild animals come to drink."

"How many bedrooms?" Warren asked.

James answered, "Three bedrooms, three bathrooms. Here are some pictures of the home. The back of the house overlooks the pool and the jungle. As you can see, the house is in an *L* shape, with floor-to-ceiling windows in the back of the house. There are curtains that can be drawn when needed. And it comes fully furnished. All you truly have to do is move in. If you want, your option, it comes with a caretaker who lives on the estate."

"What is the price?" Warren asked.

"$600,000," James replied.

"Does it have a state-of-the-art security system?" Warren asked.

"No," said James, "but our staff can add it."

"Good," said Warren. "Could you add the same security systems I have in my Massapequa home?"

"Yes, of course," said James, "but there will be additional fees."

"How long would it take to install the security system?" Warren asked.

"It shouldn't take more than five days. Probably three to five days," James said.

"Try to make it three instead of five," Warren replied.

"I can try, but I can't promise that. We want it done so it works," James stated.

"Fine," said Warren. "Please draw up the papers. If you need a deposit to hold the house, ask Raúl to wire it to you, and I will pay in full for everything else at the closing, assuming all the work is done to my satisfaction."

"That's fine, and thank you," replied James.

"Good. I have to get back to my painting now. Stop by if there is anything else you need to discuss with me. Adios."

Warren shook James's hand and left to go back to the master bedroom to continue painting. Sofia and James spoke briefly, and then James left.

An hour later, Sofia knocked on the bedroom door to see how Warren was doing.

"Hi, Warren. I just wanted to know if I can get you anything. Coffee, tea, or a snack of some sort?"

"What I would really like is a cappuccino. Do you have that here?"

"Yes, of course," Sofia said. "I will be back with it in a little while."

"Thanks," said Warren.

A little while later, Sofia returned with a cup of cappuccino. As she opened the door, Warren said, "You have great timing. I just finished."

"Yes, I see," Sofia said. "Why is the painting so dark? It looks like a beach scene with palm trees and hammock with the ocean waves in the background."

"The name of the painting is *Love Lost*," said Warren.

"Oh," said Sofia, "judging from all the darkness, it must have been a terrible loss."

"It was," Warren replied. "She was a beautiful woman—tall, blonde hair, kind, loving, a good listener, and a great deal of fun."

"Then what happened?" asked Sofia in a voice so soft and low, almost afraid to ask the question.

"Cancer," said Warren. "Colon cancer. We didn't catch it in time. She hated to go to the doctor. The painting initially didn't have the darkness in it. It was, like you said, a beach scene. That's where we met."

"Where did you meet?" asked Sofia.

"On Bagni di Tiberio, a beach on the island of Capri. In English, it means the 'beach of the emperor.' She was swimming among the ruins of an ancient Roman villa. There was a glow around her, and I knew at once I was in love. We married two years later. Everything was going great. The world was our oyster when she took ill, and the rest went too fast."

Sofia could see Warren was still in love with his deceased wife. "So you just painted over the palm trees and hammock in black to remember her," stated Sofia.

"Yes," answered Warren.

"What was her name?" asked Sofia.

"Dominique," replied Warren. "And do you know the definition of Dominique?"

Sofia said, "No."

"Dominique as a first name means 'unique and special.' She was very bright and a natural singer. She was adorable, but you don't ever want to be on her wrong side. She was too shy to strike up a conversation, but she was a great observer. I couldn't ever hide anything from her. Bottom line, she was my best friend." Sofia realized as Warren continued with the definition of Dominique that he was actually describing his wife, and as he described her, a smile came over his face.

Sofia thought, *Wow, what a love*, and she truly understood why Warren named the painting *Love Lost*. It truly captured the moment and meaning of the picture.

Warren sipped the cappuccino and said, "My work is done. Let's go out for dinner tonight, and tomorrow let's explore the neighborhood."

'Sure," replied Sofia. "I know a nice Italian place not far from the house, but early tomorrow afternoon, Raul's plane will arrive here to take you back to Mexico City."

The time to leave for the plane came quicker than expected. On the way to the airport, Warren thought, *The weekend went too fast. But considering all the accomplishments, it was an amazing success.*

As they pulled into the hangar, Warren spotted James, walked over to him, and asked when he could move into his new home.

James replied, "By Wednesday, the security system you requested will be installed. On Thursday or Friday, I will do a walk-through of the home to make sure all items are done to specifications. So the closing could take place Friday afternoon."

"Good," Warren replied. "Thanks for all your help. Keep me posted on the walk-through and closing date."

Warren entered the plane and was met by Phyllis, Chuck, and José, the same crew that had flown him down. Phyllis asked, "Any luggage?"

"Just the two paintings and my backpack," replied Warren.

"Okay, buckle up. We will be leaving shortly," Phyllis said as she sat down and buckled up. Shortly it was, as Warren buckled up, Chuck taxied the plane slowly out of the hangar; and in no time, they were in the air.

As Warren was walking off the plane in Mexico City, he spotted the driver who had taken him to the airport. The driver motioned to him, and Warren was about to get in the limo when Phyllis called to him, "Don't forget the paintings!" Warren headed back to the plane, and Phyllis met him at the bottom of the stairs, handed them to him, and wished him good luck with the auction. Warren smiled and again walked toward the driver and the limo.

As Warren got into the limo, the driver asked, "So how did you like Puerto Aventuras?"

"Oh, it was great," Warren replied.

"Good to hear," the driver stated. "Raúl has instructed me to drop you off at the auction house and for you to head to the guest rooms above the gallery. He also mentioned that he would call you tonight to make sure all is ready for tomorrow." When they got to the auction house, the driver pulled up the garage door and opened the door leading to the guest rooms. He carried Warren's two paintings into the room and placed them on top of the table in the middle of the living room. He gave Warren a quick tour of the room and said, "Good night. I hope you get a good rest for tomorrow."

Warren smiled and thanked him as he handed Warren the key.

Several hours later, Raúl called. "Buenas tardes, Warren. How was your stay at my home in Puerto Aventuras?"

"It was great," said Warren. "I got the two paintings done and purchased a home. A productive weekend, I would say."

"Yes," said Raúl. "I heard about the purchase from James. I told him no deposit was needed, so when you close, you will have to pay the entire price. By the way, I transferred 51 million to your US bank account. The balance, 3 million, is still in my account and can be transferred to your account in the US, but I wasn't sure how much would be needed for your new home."

"That's fine," said Warren. "But can you call James and get an exact figure so that tomorrow you can wire back to America all the money except the amount for the closing?"

"Yes," said Raúl. "So you want me to hold the money for the closing on your new home?"

"Yes," said Warren.

"Okay, that is no problem, Warren." Then Raúl asked, "Are you happy with the paintings?"

"Yes, very," answered Warren.

"What is the name of the painting we are auctioning off tomorrow?"

"*Clouds over Mexico City*," Warren replied.

"Okay," Raúl said. "Get some sleep. We have a lot to do tomorrow."

"Agreed. Good night," Warren said and hung up the phone.

At 11:00 a.m. the next day, there was a knock at Warren's door. Not sure if he should answer it, he called out, "Who is it?"

"Señor, Señor Diaz sent me to tell you to come down to the auction room soon. It's almost noon."

"Okay, thank you. Tell Señor Diaz I will be down in thirty minutes," Warren said.

At eleven thirty, Warren went down to the auction room. His stomach was in knots as he waited for the auction to begin. He just wanted it to be over.

As the painting was being hung on the wall, Raúl walked over to Warren and commented that he liked the clouds and that he saw the elephants and several other animals and people. "You know, Warren, you have talent. This painting is very imaginative and colorful. Are you sure you don't have any other paintings you want to sell?"

"No," Warren said quickly. "I just want to get this over with and get back to the States." But as Warren took another deep breath, he began to calm down, and he said to Raúl, "Listen, once I get to my new home, I'm sure I will have extra time for painting. I'll give you a call to arrange a private viewing. Do we have a deal?"

"Of course," Raúl said without hesitation. "You have real talent. I would love to be your agent."

Warren just laughed and shrugged his shoulders.

It was noon, and the auctioneer banged his gavel to bring the room to order. There were only six people in the room, and Warren thought, *Raúl promised only his employees would be in the place, so there would be no screwups.*

The auctioneer started to describe the painting. "This one is titled *Clouds over Mexico City*."

As the auctioneer continued, Raúl came up to Warren and said, "This just came for you."

Warren looked at the package and started to open it up. It was a new cell phone from Steven, with a note that said, "Take the SIM card out of the old phone then destroy the old phone then destroy the SIM card. This new phone is active, and the three new numbers are in your contacts list. Other developments have occurred. Will fill you in when you get back home."

Raúl was looking over Warren's shoulder as Warren read the note. "Anything wrong?" asked Raúl.

"No. Usual business stuff," answered Warren, and then he sent Steven a text: "Got phone. Call u later."

"Raúl," Warren asked, "are all these people your people?"

"Yes," said Raúl. Warren and Raúl turned toward the front, as they heard the auctioneer getting started.

"Who will start the bidding on *Clouds over Mexico City* at $20 million?" Immediately, someone bid 23 million, and another paddle was raised after that. As the bidding continued, Warren felt confident that there weren't going to be any surprises this time, so he went for a cup of coffee.

As he walked back into the auction room with his coffee, the auctioneer was just saying, "$50 million going once, going twice—"

Before he could finish the count, from the back of the room, a man shouted, "55!" As the man walked forward, Warren immediately noticed it was Diaz, the cartel representative.

"Brother," Diaz said, "did you think we wouldn't stop by and help you with your little problem?"

"Little problem? I don't know what you're talking about. Raúl convinced me I have talent and I could make a significant amount of money with him as my agent, so I put him to the test. I guess he can spot talent." Warren was trying to mask his discomfort; not knowing why Diaz had dropped by only made him more uncomfortable.

"Mr. Diaz, how will you be paying for the painting?" asked the auction clerk.

"I will give you a check for 5 million, and the balance has been wired into your account.

The clerk looked at Raúl for direction as to what to do. Raúl said, "That is correct." The clerk made notes and walked away with the check. Diaz put his arm around Warren and pulled him in close, squeezing tightly, and said, "The businessmen that I represent want to thank you for all your help in the recent agreement, and they authorized me to pay Raul's fee. We are paying Raúl's fee. Do you understand?"

"No, but business is business." Warren got close to Diaz and said quietly, "And if you ever touch me again, I will drop you where you stand. Do *you* understand?"

Diaz looked into Warren's face and saw how pissed he was. Warren took a step away and said, "Remember, respect begets respect. Force begets greater force." Warren smiled and walked away.

"Where is Señor Raúl?" he asked an employee.

The employee replied, "I will get him, Señor."

"Raúl, I would have appreciated a heads-up. What the fuck is going on? Why is he here?"

"Warren," Raúl explained, "I apologize for my associate. He was sent here to pay my fee. I believe it is truly a thank-you. At least that's the message I got. However, I did not expect anyone else to show up. My understanding was that I was to bill them for my 10 percent auction fee."

"Okay," Warren said. "Has the money been wired to my account in New York?"

Raúl said, "James told me he thinks the total cost will be $1.2 million. If it is okay, I want to hold $1.5 million. That way, if there is anything else you need for your new home, you have money in this country to take care of it."

"That's fine, but transfer the rest now," said Warren, still fuming from the unexpected visit by Diaz.

Raúl motioned to the clerk and asked if the balance of the money could be wired to Warren's account.

"Yes," the clerk said, "but it won't show up in the account until tomorrow."

"Wait," said Warren. "Can you wire $20,000,000 to the feds and $2,000,000 to New York State for income tax?"

The clerk nodded. "Good," replied Warren. "Then wire the balance to my account in New York."

Warren looked at Raul and asked, "When can I leave, and where is the *Love Lost* painting?"

"My car is waiting for you. The painting is in the car, and the plane is ready to leave as soon as you arrive," Raúl answered.

Warren turned to Raúl, shook his hand, and said, "Thank you for your hospitality, and when you are in Puerto Aventuras, you are welcome to come and visit me." They both laughed. Warren hugged Raúl and told him quietly, "Hope to see you soon," and proceeded to walk to the waiting limo.

As Warren got into the limo, the driver said, "We will be at the airport in ten minutes, and the pilot radioed me that they have clearance to leave as soon as you arrive."

"Great," Warren responded. As soon as he climbed into the plane, it took off.

CHAPTER 14

When they landed at Republic Airport in Farmingdale, Steven was there to pick Warren up.

"How did you know when I was going to land?" Warren asked.

"Rock Mama," Steven replied.

"Huh?" Warren didn't understand how she could possibly know.

"She got a call from the pilot. Apparently, he had purchased his engagement ring from her. It's a small world."

"Yeah, it's really a small world," Warren agreed. Suddenly, Warren yelled out nervously, "Stop! Stop! My car is here."

"No, it isn't," said Steven. "Maryann and I picked it up when I heard the trip to Mexico would be longer than expected. Your car is home."

Warren relaxed, and then he asked Steven, "Okay, what's the full story on Caroline?"

"Caroline's boyfriend, Jonathan, started asking questions all around Massapequa to find out who was supplying Caroline with her drugs. He's been seen a couple times at the seventh precinct and was asking questions of park people and town employees about drug dealers."

"Did Maryann stop all interaction like I asked?"

"Yes," Steven said, "but she is concerned."

"What is the timeline on the Eagle's Nest project? When will they be done?" Warren asked.

"Black Ops told me the security in the tunnels and other modifications will not be done for four to six weeks. The security for the houses and property won't be ready for one week. So we can move in now, but our security requirements won't be active yet."

"Why?" Warren asked.

"They don't want just to install it. They want it to work," Steven said.

"Those are the same words James from Puerto Aventuras used when I asked him about installing the security system in Casa Selva," Warren said.

Steven asked, "What's Casa Selva? I assume it is a house in Puerto Aventuras?"

"Yes," Warren answered. "It is a house. I figured that Eagle's Nest wouldn't be ready, so I bought Casa Selva to live in, in the meantime. It is also a great place to escape the winters of Idaho."

"How much?" Steven asked.

"Nothing," replied Warren with a big smile. "I used the proceeds of the sale of my first painting."

Steven's eyes opened wide.

"Oh," Warren continued, "I have pictures on my phone. It has three bedrooms and three bathrooms and a cave."

"And who is the third bedroom for?" Steven asked, laughing.

Warren's answer was "Friends, of course."

As they pulled into the driveway of their home, Warren said, "It is good to be home."

Steven said to Warren as they entered the kitchen, "You should call Maryann to let her know you are home and invite her over."

"Good idea." Warren picked up his cell and called her right away. "Hi, Maryann. I'm home. How are you doing? Come over so we can discuss everything. See you in ten minutes." As he hung up his cell phone, Warren turned to Steven and said, "You're right. She seemed anxious."

There was a knock on the door, and Warren yelled, "Come in, Maryann!"

Maryann opened the door and said, "You let me in without checking who was at the door. Some security."

"Wrong. It was security that let us know it was you. As you drove in the driveway, your plate was checked. And as you got out of your car, facial-recognition software confirmed who you were. By the time you reached the door, we knew it was you and that you were alone. That security comes with the home you purchased. Feel better now?"

"No," Maryann said. "This Caroline thing has me freaking out."

"Okay," Warren said. "Let's go over this. When was the last time you saw her or dealt with her?"

"Two months ago at the 7-Eleven I half-own, she had asked for Oakland A's by 2. She usually only asked for one, so I thought it was odd, but because of all the stuff that was going on back then with Diaz and MS-13, I gave her what she ordered, outside of any camera view, and went about my business."

"When did she die?" asked Warren.

Steven answered, "A week ago."

"And you had no contact with her in the last two months?" Warren asked Maryann, looking right at her.

"No, I had no contact since that last meeting," replied Maryann.

"You and I are in the clear. Let's have dinner. Do you want pizza, Chinese food, or chicken?" Warren asked Maryann.

"Who do you order the pizza from?" Maryann asked.

"Gregorio's Pizza. They have the everything crust. It's like the everything bagel. It is very tasty. The Chinese we order from Potstickers Company, delicious and always ready in fifteen minutes. Chicken Au Go Go for fried chicken, and you can get side orders there. However, Chicken Au Go Go we have to pick up. So what is your pleasure?"

"Pizza," Maryann said.

"Great," answered Warren. "Steven, please order two pies, both with the everything crust. One plain and the other half-mushroom and half-sausage. I want to take a shower before the food gets here. Thanks."

"Maryann, do you want a glass of wine?" Steven asked.

"Sure," Maryann answered.

"Red or white?"

"Red, please," Maryann answered.

"Fine. One glass of red wine coming up," replied Steven.

Warren walked into the room still drying his hair, wearing shorts and a polo shirt. The security system announced, "You have an unidentified visitor. Prepared and armed."

"Maryann, check this out." Warren waved her to come over to the computer screen in the kitchen. "This is how we knew it was you. Baby Blue, it is the pizza delivery man. Cancel alert."

The security system responded, "Alert canceled."

When the doorbell rang, Maryann was a little amused to hear that it was "The Song of the Marines." Warren paid the delivery man for the pizza and told him to have a good night.

"Come, let's sit in the dining room," Warren said. Steven got the glasses and the bottle of wine. Everyone took a slice and began eating right away. Steve finished first and went for a second slice, this time a mushroom slice. Warren picked up a second sausage slice, and before he bit into it, he looked at Maryann and asked, "Are you still willing to buy the house and the businesses?"

At the moment, Maryann had a mouthful, so she didn't respond. For those few seconds, Warren's faced shown his concern. After all, his future plans all depended on her buying the house and the businesses and running it so the cartel would stay off his back.

Maryann finally swallowed, smiled, and said, "Yes, still on track and still willing to close on the agreed date and time."

Warren answered, "Great!"

"Now that I see the security system you have here, I want to move here ASAP. Will the system need any reprogramming once I move in? And by the way, who is Baby Blue?" Maryann asked.

Steven replied, "Yes, but it's not difficult. Usernames, passwords, safe words will all have to be changed, and you are going to have to understand the protocols. With your background, you won't have any problems."

"And Baby Blue?" she asked again.

"Baby Blue is the name I gave to the security system," Steven replied, as Warren smirked.

"Is there more to the system than I saw?" asked Maryann.

Steven smiled and said, "Yes, a lot more."

Warren added, "This is Steven's baby. He designed it because he wanted to feel secure in this house. We were told by Black Ops that the system Steven designed was sold to the White House and is being used there and at all the US embassies around the world. He got a sizable commission check for that."

"Not to brag," Steven continued, "but Black Ops told me another check is coming. Britain just purchased it for their embassies."

"Okay, bottom line—next Friday, we will have a closing, just the three of us and our attorneys. All-cash transaction. You probably should have an attorney, just to make sure all the titles are changed."

Maryann asked, "Do you know any?"

Warren answered, "Just look at the Massapequa Chamber's member list, but I know Leff and Leff or Ballato Law—they do real estate transactions. But you should meet with them and decide which one you are the most comfortable with."

Steven got up from the table and walked to the kitchen and asked, "Does anyone want coffee?"

"Cappuccino for me," Warren stated.

"Same for me," answered Maryann.

"Three cappuccinos coming right up," Steven replied.

"What are you two going to do?" Maryann asked.

Warren said, "I just purchased a place in Mexico, Casa Selva. It is a thirty-minute drive into the jungle to the villa from the highway. I want to paint. I'm finding it therapeutic, and I thought about writing a book about a gang of guys that turn into a brotherhood of men watching out for one another, no questions asked. But most importantly, it is time for me to retire. My father taught me, if you no longer have what it takes to be successful, leave. He said it was better to leave a little from the top than being asked to leave."

"What did your father do?" asked Maryann.

"He was a corporate executive for a major US company. He left while on top and was given a large consulting contract. But he learned a lot climbing the corporate ladder. He did it the old-fashioned way—performance and integrity. But he always had time for his kids, a great sense of humor, and a positive outlook on life."

"What will Steven do?"

"Steven, as long as he has access to the internet, he can do business from anywhere. He established the security business because of what he wanted in our security system for this house. He is smart enough to design the software and to implement his designs. He is an accountant by trade. So if you have questions about the system, he is the best to explain it. Black Ops has placed him on retainer to enhance the system or solve problems with it. One of the conditions of the contract was his existence could never be acknowledged. So the jungle is an excellent place for him. Black Ops tells everyone it is a group of ex-military people in Idaho who came up with it. If he never gets another check, he is set."

"Cappuccino for three," Steven said as he brought in a tray of cookies and cappuccinos. "What have you guys been talking about? My ears were ringing."

"Yes, it was all about you, Steven, your genius with security software and ability to balance my books," Warren answered.

"Good cappuccino," Maryann said, hoping to change the subject. "But seriously, how long will it take to master the security system?"

Steven replied with a smile like a father talking about a son. "Almost all the system is based on voice commands and your understanding of the force that is under your command. You must understand what it can't or won't do. The rest it does automatically. That is the reason it has been so well-received by the countries and companies that have purchased it. For the most part, the people it protects aren't professionals. They are mostly civilians. Oh, you need to pick a name for the system—something simple but different enough and something you will always remember."

"Yes, but how long?" Maryann asked again.

"In a day, you will have it down pat," Steven answered.

"When do we get started?" Maryann asked.

"Friday, right after the closing. If it's okay, I'll stay over the garage, in the bonus room, until all is changed over and you are comfortable with the system," Steven replied.

"Good," Maryann said. "That makes me feel better, knowing you will be here until I get the hang of it. Will you be here too, Warren?"

"No," Warren said. "I'm off to do a walk-through and then a closing on Casa Selva, our new home in Mexico. Maryann, when do you want to start moving your stuff in?"

"Wednesday," Maryann replied.

"Okay, then Steven and I will move all our stuff to the garage and the bonus room so you can start moving in," replied Warren.

"And remember, those paintings are staying. By the way, one is missing. The one with the palm trees and hammock. Where is it?" asked Maryann.

"Yes, I took it to get a new frame. The old one was coming apart," Warren said as he walked to his bedroom to get the painting. He brought the painting back into the dining room and hung it back on the wall.

Later that night, after Maryann left, Steven asked Warren, "Where the hell did you get that frame?"

"Raúl's driver," Warren said. "Right before the plane took off, he placed this package on the flight and said, 'Raúl thought you might need this.' Steven, can you check the frame for any type of device?"

"Anything specific?" asked Steven.

"No, I'm just not sure why he did that. This frame isn't cheap. Do a complete analysis of it. Maybe the answer is in the frame?"

"Okay, I understand," Steven replied.

Several hours later, Steven yelled out to Warren, "Good news! There are no bugging devices, and there's nothing else except wood in or on the frame. Maybe Raúl was simply being nice. You did just make him a lot of money."

"Yeah, maybe so. Okay, thanks."

When Caroline's story came out in the *Massapequa Post*, Neil called George right away. "Good morning, Neil. What's up?" asked George.

"I was reading the *Post* this morning and the story about Caroline. Could she be the lady in the white bathing suit?" asked Neil.

"I'm pretty sure it is, but I wasn't close enough to see her face. But she fits the profile," answered George. "What did you think of the article? Did it provide any new information?"

"You haven't read it?" asked Neil.

"Not yet," replied George. "I'm working on a big employee-dishonesty case for an insurance company."

"That expert-witness stuff," replied Neil.

"Well, did it provide any new information, more than what we already know?" asked George.

"No," Neil responded, "but it was well-written."

"Okay, call me next week. After this trial, I will have more time to discuss this."

"Will do. Talk to you then."

CHAPTER 15

Wednesday came, and Maryann knocked on the door early to start moving in her stuff. Warren and Steven had all their personal furniture moved to Casa Selva, and they spent all of Wednesday and Thursday helping Maryann set up the place as she wanted it. Three of them were inseparable for the two days, hanging artwork, painting walls, and having all their meals together.

On Friday, the three met in the lawyer's office to complete the real estate transaction. A bank representative was there to wire the funds from Maryann's account into Warren's account. Once the papers were signed, Warren thanked everyone and left in a waiting car to go catch his flight with Hopscotch Air back to Puerto Aventuras to close on Casa Selva.

When Warren arrived at Puerto Aventuras, he was met at the airport by James, who quickly took him through security and into a waiting car that drove them to Casa Selva. As they turned off the highway down the dirt road, Warren asked James, "How long is it from the road to the house? James said thirty minutes, but it looks longer."

"Warren," James said, "your property is gated. It is ten minutes from that gate to your home by car. From the road to your house, it is a good thirty minutes. Stop here," James said to the driver. James continued with, "Warren, at this period, we are five minutes into the drive. Ahead, there are two roadways. The straight one is the one that leads to a dead end and a swamp the invaders will sink into. There is no path out of there. If you keep right on this road, you will reach your casa. Also, from the air, you can't see a path to your casa. We have also installed sensors on the ground on the entire property for a variety of reasons." The two got out of the car to inspect the roadway, and James showed Warren what the sensors looked like. The temperature under the shady trees was much cooler than when they left the airport.

James continued, "The variety of reasons are…well, the first one is obvious—unwanted visitors. But secondly, a guest could get lost. You can track their footsteps through the sensors. And lastly, there are wild monkeys, ocelots, jaguar, deer, and coati on this property, and we have wired the system to alert you if any of them get close to the casa. Basically, any footsteps, just like your system at home, are going to be checked against your guest visitors. This property has cameras to make it easy to do surveillance of the entire property, and each camera overlaps another part of the property. In case one camera is taken out, the two other cameras can see what is going on in that sector."

"So each area is surveilled by cameras and ground sensors, and it is thirty minutes before anyone gets to the house?" Warren asked.

"Correct," James replied. "Now let's drive through the gate. There is another layer of protection here." As they drove down the road through the gate, James asked the driver to stop again and got out, motioning to Warren to do the same. As Warren got out, James asked him, "What do you think of the gate?"

"What gate?" Warren asked.

"Your brother came up with this idea for an embassy in the Brazil jungle. Former Disney engineers created the trees. Once you arm the system, these trees are deadly. They have more firepower than a tank and create a nearly impenetrable wall."

"Nice," Warren said. "And from this point, it is ten minutes to the front door."

"Yes," said James.

They both got back into the car, and Warren said to James, "What is really amazing about that gate is you can't detect that it was just built. It looks as if Mother Nature created it."

James replied, "The inspiration was Mother Nature, but only Disney engineers could improve on her design." They both laughed.

As they drove into the parking area of the home, James told Warren that they had built a safe room in the house. "The safe room is off the master bedroom, and inside it are the master controls for the security system, and off the kitchen is the other access point for the security system. But when you alarm the safe room, the system in the kitchen shuts down."

As they both walked into the safe room, Warren studied the view of all the twenty-eight cameras. The room was a large room with four bunk beds. It looked like it had been stocked with enough food and water for a month. There was a bathroom and a game table that could be easily flipped to become a dining table.

James reached over to the security console and flipped three switches. "These," he said, "are for the three cameras hidden on the roof. Each can be turned to view different areas, so on the off chance the jungle cameras turn off, you still have these to show you what is going on outside. These switches also activate the hidden gun turrets, just like the system at your Massapequa home. This last switch is to arm the wall."

"Excellent," Warren said, then he inspected the ability of the cameras to see what was going on outside. "You're right. The cameras do overlap, but what is the exit strategy from the safe room?"

James pointed to a door on the floor. "This door goes down almost thirteen meters, or fifteen feet, to a tunnel that goes to the sea." Warren bent down, opened the door, and climbed down into the tunnel. James followed him. As he got down to the floor of the tunnel, Warren asked, "What keeps the lights on down here?"

James replied, "The lights go on when the door opens. Once you close the door, the lights go out, and there is a switch here to turn them back on. Once the switch down here is turned on, the door upstairs is locked." Warren and James walked through the tunnel and ended up on the bluffs overlooking the sea twenty minutes later. James handed Warren an electronic key and said, "Warren, the buttons on this key lock or unlock the doors in your casa. The blue button locks or opens the entrance to the tunnel in the safe room. The red button locks the safe-room door. You also can lock it manually. In the bedroom, there is an iPad set up to pick up any alarms or movements on the property. I will also set the system up to notify your cell phone at the same time."

"Okay," Warren said. "Everything looks good. Let's get to the closing."

James took out his phone and called the driver to pick them up on the beach. Within the hour, they were back at the Black Ops office to close on the Casa Selva property.

CHAPTER 16

Several hours later, Warren was back at Casa Selva, enjoying his first swim in the pool, when he heard his cell phone ring. He was getting out of the pool when a man, about five foot ten, with a big smile and a muscular body brought his cell phone to him.

"Good evening. My name is Mateo. I'm part of the staff that comes with the casa. Your phone, Señor."

"Oh, thank you." Warren looked at the phone and saw it was Steven.

"Hey, Steven, what's up?" Warren asked.

"Nothing. All good here. Just helping Maryann get used to the system," Steven replied. "And you?"

"Casa Selva is ours. I closed on it today. That wall is an excellent idea," Warren said.

"I thought you would like that," Steven replied.

"So when are you going to be ready to come down?" Warren asked.

"Hopefully, in a couple days," Steven replied.

"Okay, good. I'll call you back later. There is a guy named Mateo here who said he comes with the casa, so I want to find out about the staff that comes with the place. Okay, bye," Warren said and hung up.

"Mateo!" Warren called out.

Mateo walked out the kitchen door into the pool area and said, "Yes, Señor Warren?"

"Mateo, I was unaware that the casa came with staff. James mentioned that staff could be hired, but he didn't mention that one was already in place."

"We served the former owners," Mateo stated. "James asked me to come by tonight to make sure you were okay and getting used to your new casa."

"How many are there?" Warren asked.

"Three, Señor. Myself, I cook and do repairs; my wife, who cooks and cleans the casa; and Rick, who is in charge of all the landscape and the electronic systems that go along with that. Basically, my wife and I take care of the casa, and Rick takes care of the grounds."

"Who is here now?" Warren asked.

"Just me," responded Mateo. "Did you have any dinner?"

"No," Warren replied.

"Okay, I will fix you something. Would you like a sandwich or a hot meal?"

"A sandwich and something to drink would be great, thanks," Warren said. When Mateo walked back into the kitchen, Warren picked up his cell phone and called James.

"Hey, James, this is Warren."

"How's everything going at your new casa?" asked James.

Warren cut him off, "James, did you send a guy named Mateo to check on me?"

"Yes," James said.

"Describe him," Warren said.

"He's very tall and built like a bouncer with a big smile," said James.

"Okay, that's him, but why didn't you tell me?" asked Warren.

"I didn't want you to feel obligated to him and his family. They live about a mile down the highway, and they have cared for the house ever since it was built," James said. "If you don't want him there, I will tell him to leave."

"No, that's not necessary. He's making me a sandwich right now, but no more surprises. I don't like surprises. Always phone me first."

"Understood," said James, and then he asked, "By the way, do you need anything?"

"No," replied Warren.

"Over the garage," James continued, "there are staff quarters that consist of two bedrooms, a bathroom, and a living room. They

118

use it only on the nights they work late, instead of walking through the jungle and the highway. They sleep there and leave in the morning, if they aren't needed the next day. Are you okay with him staying tonight? I don't want Mateo walking home tonight."

"Yeah, it is okay for him to stay the night, but his sandwich better taste great," Warren said with a laugh.

"It will," said James. "He used to be the Four Seasons head chef and does all our catering."

"Good night," Warren said and hung up the phone.

"Señor Warren, your sandwich is ready," Mateo said. "And I made you American coffee."

"Thank you. James just confirmed that you and your family have taken care of this home since it was built and that there are sleeping quarters for you above the garage. So if you want to, you can stay there tonight," Warren said.

"Thank you," said Mateo.

Warren took a couple bites of the sandwich then turned to Mateo and said, "This is a great sandwich."

Mateo just gave Warren a big smile.

Warren finished the sandwich and asked Mateo, "Are you going to be around tomorrow?"

"Yes," Mateo said.

"Good. Could you take me on a walking tour of the property so I can get the full lay of the land?"

"Sure. What time tomorrow?" Mateo replied.

"Ten a.m., right after breakfast," Warren replied.

"Fine. See you tomorrow. Do you want me to cook breakfast for you?" Mateo asked.

"Yes, please," Warren responded, and as he walked toward the master bedroom, he said, "Good night, Mateo."

Warren got to the room and called Steven back.

Steven asked, "Is everything okay?"

"Yeah," replied Warren. "This guy Mateo who showed up, James had told him to stop by, but I just wasn't sure, so I called James to confirm who he was. He checked out, and he is a great cook, little brother. He may replace you from the cooking detail."

"Great, I look forward to that moment," Steven said with excitement. "I can easily fill that time up, and honestly, Black Ops is telling me that they have three or four jobs coming in that need new designs. So I may fly down so I can get my work done and let him cook. Are there other staff?"

"Yes. Mateo and his wife take care of the house, and this guy Rick takes care of the grounds. James told me there are sensors in the ground everywhere, so I imagine if they break, Rick is in charge of fixing them," Warren answered.

"Any other surprises?" Steven asked.

"No," answered Warren. "The closing went smoothly. The wire transfer went through to the Black Ops that was in the US. I'm sure that will confuse the IRS and the state taxation department. Any update on Eagle's Nest?"

"Yes, I got an email from the project manager stating he may be done a week early. The weather is holding off, so they are still plowing ahead to get the job done and all systems activated ASAP for now. It is three weeks away. I got the impression that it may be done in another week, if the weather holds off."

"Good," Warren answered. "But it doesn't matter. Casa Selva is up and running, so when can you get down here? I'm not comfortable with you up there because I'm getting a feeling things are closing in."

"I hear you and understand," Steven answered, "but I have to make sure Maryann understands and can operate the system once I leave. I don't want to have to fly back to reeducate her because if your feelings are right, and they usually are, that would be the worst time to come back. So bottom line, a week."

"Okay, fine," Warren responded, but Steven could tell he wasn't happy with his response. "Talk to you tomorrow."

CHAPTER 17

At 8:00 a.m., Warren heard a ringing alarm coming from the iPad in the bedroom, so he ran to check out what the alarm was. When he hit the screen, he saw a woman walking on the property with shopping bags and then saw Mateo walking to the woman and taking the bags from her. *It must be his wife,* Warren thought. Twenty-five minutes later, the iPad alarm went off. Again the picture on the iPad was of Mateo and his wife at the front door, even before they rang the bell.

Warren opened the door, and Mateo said, "Good morning. This is my wife, Dori. We are here to cook you breakfast and give you a tour of your property or, as you say, 'get the lay of the land.'"

Dori said, "I'm here to clean and water the plants. He's here to cook." They all laughed. Mateo went to the kitchen with Warren, and Dori went out to the pool area to check the flowers.

After breakfast, Mateo and Warren went out to survey the property.

"Mateo, James told me you've taken care of this property since it was built. What happened to the previous owners?" asked Warren.

"They were expelled. They broke the rules that safeguard this community, so the community purchased the property at market value and moved them out. I believe they moved to Chile, or at least that is where they requested their belongings be sent. Do you have any questions on the property?" asked Mateo.

"Yes, where are the caves, and how do I get to them from here?" Warren asked.

"The caves are behind the house. This way." Mateo motioned to Warren. About twenty minutes later, they were walking in the caves. Warren saw lots of different animal tracks in the ground and asked

Mateo what animal made them. Mateo bent down over the tracks and knew what each one was. "See this print here?" Mateo said.

"Which one?" asked Warren.

"This one right here." Mateo pointed to it with his finger. "Take a good look at it because it is an ocelot footprint. Four toes above the pad. Just like a domestic cat paw print but much bigger. They prey on small animals. You don't have any dogs, do you?" asked Mateo.

"No," said Warren. "Can I hunt on my property?"

"Yes," Mateo said, "but only for deer, and you need a permit from the government."

As they were walking, Mateo's cell phone rang. It was Dori, so he answered it. They only spoke briefly, and then Mateo said to Warren, "Okay, we should head back now."

"Why?" Warren asked.

"Dori said your cell phone has been ringing. We should head back."

They turned around and headed toward the house. When they got back, Dori handed Warren his cell phone and told him, "You should keep this with you. You never know when you're going to need it."

Warren smiled and said, "Very true." Then he phoned Steven. "Hi, Steven. You called?"

"Yes. Maryann got it. I gave her the certification test for the security system, and she passed, 100 percent."

"Great," said Warren. "Call Doug at Hopscotch Air in Republic. I'll text you his number. Tell him you need a flight to Puerto Aventuras. He knows what to do. You need to pack the rest of our stuff and bring it down here."

"Already started, and I will be done this afternoon," said Steven.

"Okay, can you leave tonight?" asked Warren.

"Yes, I probably can be ready to leave by six thirty," Steven stated.

"Okay, that means you'll probably get here by ten thirty p.m. I'll meet you at the airport," responded Warren.

"Good. See you then. Bye," Steven replied.

"I imagine that call was urgent, Señor Warren," said Dori.

"Yes. It was my brother. He is coming down. He'll be here about ten thirty or eleven o'clock," replied Warren.

"Okay, I'll make sure his room is ready," Dori said.

Time seemed to fly by. It was 10:00 p.m.—already time to drive to the airport to pick up Steven. As Warren was getting into his car, Mateo said, "Do you want me to come with you to help with the luggage?"

"That's a good idea. Sure, hop in," replied Warren. By the time Warren and Mateo reached the airport, the plane had landed and was pulling into the hangar.

As the plane door opened, Phyllis walked down the stairs and yelled, "Hey, Warren!" James was at the security entrance, and when he heard Phyllis say Warren's name, he turned to find Warren and gave him a thumbs-up. The crew had disembarked, and Steven stood at the doorway, waiting to get waved down from the security guard. As he started down the stairs, the hangar crew began to unload the plane.

Steven reached James, and James said, "Warren's brother, I presume."

"Yes, I'm Steven."

"Your luggage is being unloaded and will be delivered to your car. No use in you waiting here," said James.

Warren and Steven finally met and gave each other a big hug and a high five. "Finally. Good to see you down here," said Warren and then introduced Mateo. After the hangar crew brought Steven's luggage to the car, Mateo started to pack the bags into the car.

"All done," Mateo said, and the three of them piled into the car and left for the trip home. Forty-five minutes later, they were back at Casa Selva.

"Wow," Steven said. "This is nice."

"Wait until morning," Warren said, "and you get to check out the property and the water." Mateo started taking the luggage from the car to Steven's room. Warren and Steven walked through to the pool. The pool lights were on, and the house reflected in the pool. The house lights also lit up the jungle surrounding the house.

"You were right. We are in the jungle," said Steven.

"Yep. We are thirty minutes from the highway. Anything new on the Caroline or Maryann's problems?" Warren asked.

"No, but I think you are right. Things seem to be closing in on her," Steven replied.

"Is she in trouble?" asked Warren with a concerned voice.

"No, not now, but things are getting more difficult with MS-13 and the cartel," Steven answered.

"Is the cartel living up to the agreement?" Warren asked.

"Yes, to the best of my knowledge. But it's not the cartel. It's—"

Warren cut him off. "MS-13 is the problem," Warren stated in an angry tone.

"You knew that was going to happen," Steven said.

"Yeah, there is nothing we can do. She's a big girl. I'm happy you are here now and not involved with that," Warren said. "But," Warren continued, "she does know she can depend on us if something goes wrong, right?"

"Yes, she knows that, but maybe you should call her?" Steven said with a little smile to tease Warren.

"Señores, we are going to retire now. Is there anything else you need?" Mateo asked.

Then Dori butted in and told Mateo to get Señor Steven a sandwich. Mateo left for the kitchen, with Warren and Steven right behind. Once in the kitchen, Dori said good night and left. Once Mateo was done making sandwiches, he said good night and asked if they would need him tomorrow.

Warren answered, "Yes. We need to get Steven's systems for his business up and running."

CHAPTER 18

About one week later, Steven received a video call from Maryann.

"Hey, Maryann," Steven greeted, but Maryann had no time for formalities.

"Steven, the system just activated, and there are two guys who just got out of a car and are walking toward the door."

"Okay, quickly point your cell phone at the screen. I might be able to ID them. Yes, the guy on the left is a Nassau County cop. I'm not sure of the guy on the right, but if they are riding together, they are probably both cops. But they should identify themselves and tell you why they are knocking on your door."

The doorbell rang, and as it was still ringing, one of the men started knocking on the door.

"One minute!" yelled Maryann.

"Maryann, tell Melvin to watch, listen, and record," Steven said. Melvin was the name Maryann had given to the security system.

"Okay, Melvin," Maryann said to the security monitor in the kitchen, "watch, listen, and record." Then she yelled again to the front door, "Coming!"

Maryann opened the door and said, "Yes, can I help you?"

The guy on the left showed his badge and said, "Good morning. I'm Barnard King, a Nassau County detective. This is my partner." The partner just smiled. "May we come in?"

"Sure," Maryann replied and stepped out of the way so they both could enter. "What is this about?"

"We are investigating the death of Caroline Roth, and we have information that you saw her before she died," said Detective King.

"She was the one whose death was reported in the *Massapequa Post*," Maryann said.

"Yes," Detective King replied. While King was looking straight at Maryann, the other detective seemed to be studying the whole house.

Maryann looked at him and said, "What are you doing? You look like you're casing my house so you can rob it. Both of you get out! I'm not comfortable with this one around." Maryann pointed to the other detective. "If you don't have warrants, get out of my house." When the detectives didn't move, Maryann started to yell, "Get out, and get out!" She watched as they walked back to their car.

As Detective King got into his car, he turned to the other cop and said, "Are all FBI agents as big an ass as you are? Christ, Wiley. You, in five minutes, creeped her out. Now what am I going to say to my supervisor?"

"Tell him she was uncooperative and she's involved," Wiley responded.

"What, are you nuts? That's not true, and it would never stand up in court," King said.

Still parked in front of the house, Wiley said, "You see that small antenna on the roof? That is a high-tech listening device. At least five cameras are surveilling the property, and they are on us right now. Do you see that bridge from the house to the top of the garage? I think there are multiple gun turrets built into the roof and the underside of the bridge."

"Wrong, Mr. FBI Man. She just bought the home about two weeks ago. The former owner was a security expert with the highest clearance from the DOD and Homeland Security," said King.

"Okay, can I now get to the MS-13 people I'm supposed to interrogate?" asked Wiley.

"Of course. You are of no help here," replied King.

Maryann had been standing in front of the kitchen monitor, listening to their conversation. As the car drove away, she couldn't move; she just stared at the screen.

"Hey, Maryann, are you still there? Maryann, are you listening? Maryann, Maryann!" Steven yelled out over the security system.

"Yes, yes," Maryann finally replied. "I was just a little creeped out by that guy."

"Okay, relax," Steven said. "They are gone, and throwing them out before they started asking questions was a great move."

Maryann interrupted, "It wasn't a move. My creep detector was on, and that guy hit all my buttons."

"Well, sister," Steven answered, "keep that creep detector on and fully charged."

They both laughed. "Sister! Really?" Maryann answered.

"Yeah, really. How long have I known you? You are the closest thing to a sister I've ever had. So yeah, sister!" Steven answered.

"Was what that guy said about the bridge correct?" asked Maryann.

"Do you mean the turrets?" asked Steven.

"Yes," answered Maryann.

"Yes, the bridge has several gun turrets built into the roof structure and the underside of the bridge. Warren had Black Ops install them before our dealings with the cartel. He felt the firepower would protect us and now you. But we went over all this. Don't you remember?"

"I guess I was overwhelmed with all the information. How do they operate again?" Maryann asked.

"By your voice command. We installed the safe room afterward, so I don't know under what circumstances you would use it. But it is active and under your voice command."

"You didn't review that part of the security system with me," Maryann stated. "Why not?"

"The system is programmed to ask you. Melvin would have asked you for the authorization to use deadly force to protect you. If you said yes, the gun turrets go live, and Melvin would ask you to identify the people on the screen whom deadly force would be used on. Once you identify them, the guns' scopes would take over. In the end, those individuals would be dead." Steven continued, "There is no real training for this part of the system. You just tell Melvin, and it is done."

"Have you ever used it?" asked Maryann.

"Yes, but not entirely. Do you remember when I called Warren the first or second time you met with the cartel and MS-13?"

"Yes, he told me to go to the safe house and stay there until he called," Maryann answered.

"Well," Steven started to answer slowly, "that night, a number of MS-13 guys were surrounding the house. The system activated the gun turrets and asked me which ones I wanted to use deadly force on. That's when I called Warren. He told me to apply maximum force to protect myself. I delayed sixty seconds, and during that time, these guys jumped back into their cars and trucks and left. And by the time Warren got here, they were gone. But the system records every incident, so we had a video of the leader and the gang members. So we know, because of that night, that the system really works. We toasted Black Ops that night. But the decision to use deadly force is yours and only yours. So, sister, I'm thrilled your creep detector is operational."

They both laughed, and then Steven said, "Let me talk to Warren, and we will get back to you."

"Good. I'm interested in hearing what Warren thinks, so I'll talk with you later?" asked Maryann.

"Yes," answered Steven. "Goodbye."

Chapter 19

The next morning, when Maryann was resetting her iPad's Wi-Fi network settings, looking for her home network in the "Choose a Network" box, as she was scrolling down, she saw a network listing that made her whole body shake. The network was called FBI SURVEILLANCE TRUCK. Maryann immediately reached for her cell phone and turned it off then turned off the iPad. Then she called Melvin.

"Yes, Maryann." Melvin's voice was modeled after Steven's voice, and it was oddly calming the moment she heard it. "You sound concerned, and I don't see any immediate threats. Are you having a health emergency?" asked Melvin.

"No," answered Maryann. "I need you to analyze the area for any electronic or Wi-Fi signal. My iPad picked up an FBI surveillance truck in the area. I need to know if we are under surveillance and by whom. Can you do that?"

"Yes, my systems can detect that if they are close to our location. And yes, you are being surveilled by that network. Should I go dark?" asked Melvin.

"What does that mean exactly?" Maryann asked.

"It is a process. First, I will strongly encrypt all forms of communication, so it looks as if you are not communicating with anyone. Secondly, I will wipe clean all the electronic devices and insert a doomsday bomb on each device, just in case they are seized. Thirdly, I will search the internet and the dark web for any record of you and change it to protect your identity, your location, and business dealings. The first two can be completed in an hour. The third could take some time, possibly a day or two."

"How do I communicate with Steven and Warren?" asked Maryann.

Melvin replied, "Go to AT&T and T-Mobile and buy two prepaid phones. When you buy them, they are already activated. Once you get them, I will give step-by-step instructions on how to use the phones so it is harder to detect you, and we may be able to communicate with Warren and Steven through the dark web."

"Can you get a secure message to Steven?" asked Maryann.

"Yes," said Melvin, "but I'll have to go through the DOD computers, so the message will have to be brief. But don't worry. Tell me what you wish to communicate, and I will get it to him."

"Tell Steven about the FBI surveillance truck and ask what I should expect and what options I have," Maryann answered.

"Fine. Will do," replied Melvin.

"Oh, Melvin," Maryann stated.

"Yes, Maryann?"

"I'm leaving to buy those prepaid phones. Keep the house armed and prevent anyone from entering the house while I'm gone. Do you understand?" Maryann asked.

"Yes, totally," Melvin replied.

"And tell me as soon as you get a reply from Steven or Warren," Maryann added as she was walking out the front door. As she closed the door and looked at the bay, she thought, *I really don't want to give up this beautiful view, but only time will tell.* She snapped back into reality and said to herself, *I've got things to pick up. I need to stop worrying about tomorrow. I need to deal with today.*

⁂

A few blocks away from Maryann's house, Jonathan was knocking on a neighbor's front door.

"Hi, I'm Jonathan, Caroline Roth's friend."

"Yes, I know who you are," said George. "How can I help you?"

"I understand that you are a detective, and I want your help to find out who killed my girlfriend," stated Jonathan.

George put up his hand to stop him from saying anything further. "I'm retired, and it is my understanding that the Nassau County Police Department is looking into your girlfriend's death."

Jonathan shot back in a more conciliatory tone, "I need your help. My girlfriend is dead, and people in the neighborhood told me you are a stand-up guy and if anyone could help, it would be you."

"I understand what you want," George replied. "But this is an active investigation, and no one will give me access to their files in an active investigation. And I think you can understand why."

"Yeah, but the guy they have on the case, a Detective Barnard King, I'm not sure he is really on the case."

"Why do you think that?" asked George.

"Because every time I ask for an update on the case, he tells me nothing new. I found out that Caroline was going to Burns Park for drugs, and I thought she had finally stopped after the last time I confronted her. But now I think she switched to getting her drugs at the 7-Eleven on Merrick Road, across from TD Bank."

"Do you have any proof?" asked George.

"Only what I found in our boat after her death," replied Jonathan.

"What did you find in your boat?"

"It was oxycodone."

"Do you still have it? Does it have any marking on it?" George asked, hoping for a yes answer. George had put on his poker face, not showing that Jonathan's info confirmed his suspicions about Burns Park. A local drug ring was, in fact, using the place as a drug drop.

"No, I got rid of it as soon as I figured out what it was," Jonathan stated.

"Do you know which drug killed your girlfriend?" asked George.

"Not sure, but I think oxycodone had something to do with Caroline's death. Shouldn't Detective King know that?" responded Jonathan.

"That's the type of info that could break open her case," George said. "Jonathan, you should have mentioned that to Detective King. Listen, I'm sorry for your loss, but I have a couple projects to complete. So have a great day and good luck."

George walked into his home and slowly closed the door, thinking about what he had just heard. Just then, Olivia asked, "What was that all about?"

"That was Jonathan, the boyfriend of the girl who overdosed, whose story was in the *Massapequa Post.*"

"Oh yeah, I remember reading that. It was a pretty sad story, but what does he want from you? You aren't going to get involved, are you?" asked Olivia.

"I told him, 'No, I'm retired,'" responded George.

"Good. Let's keep it that way. I don't want to start worrying about you investigating a high-profile drug crime *again*. I worried each day you left for work, whether you were going to come home alive. Those drug-cartel people are bad people."

George laughed. "*Bad* people? Really, they are the *worst* of criminals, and again I agree with you. I told the man I was retired and to call the detective on the case."

"Who's the detective on the case?" asked Olivia.

"King," replied George.

"George, if you know the detective handling this case, then you know a lot more than you are telling me." She turned and looked right into his face and said, "Don't give me that poker face. That guy wouldn't have come to our front door if all you knew was the detective's name, George. This time, you aren't hiding me and the kids in your friend's cabin in Upstate New York. I'm not doing that again!" Then she stormed out of the living room.

"Olivia, listen. The only reason I know the detective handling the case is that guy just told me. Relax, I'm not involved," George told her.

George walked downstairs to his office and closed the door to call Neil.

"Hey, buddy, I got some info for you," George told Neil.

"Really? About the Caroline murder?" asked Neil.

"Yep," responded George. "Jonathan was just here asking for my help in her murder."

"Oh shit. I hope you told him hell no," Neil said.

"No, I let him down easy. I told him I can't help him because I'm retired."

"Good one," Neil said. "But what did he tell you?"

"He confirmed what we suspected—there was, or is, a local drug dealer using Burns Park as a drop-off point."

Neil replied, "Because of your tip and Annie's murder, the police had been doing spot searches at the park three months before her death, and NCPD found nothing. No bags, no money, no messages, and no suspicious people around. It was dry. King told me it has been like a morgue. There's been no action since Annie's death. King doesn't think the person who gave the drugs was your ordinary drug dealer. But he wanted to interview your new neighbor, the new part-owner of the 7-Eleven. King thinks she was the last one to see her alive aside from her boyfriend. I really think that King is hoping your neighbor can shed light on her state of mind or find out if she had any interaction with her."

"Is she a suspect? And why isn't Jonathan a suspect?" George asked.

"I don't think your new neighbor is a suspect, and Jonathan has a rock-solid alibi," Neil responded. "But you know that can change."

"Neil, have you heard where the old owner went?" asked George.

"You mean Steven?" asked Neil.

"Yeah," answered George. "Does he still have DOD protection?"

"Steven and his brother left the country—something about not feeling comfortable with their personal safety. From what I understand, he still consults with DOD and the state department on security matters."

"What about his brother? What does he do?" asked George.

"He's supposedly a decorated war hero and former insurance executive who sold everything right before the market collapse in 2009 and bought it all back for pennies on the dollar. At least that's what the story is," Neil said. "But I tried to confirm all that and came up empty. The people in the insurance industry knew of him, and all said he was a great guy, but no one could confirm that he had made a killing in the market to pay for his lifestyle."

"Could he be the drug dealer?" George asked.

"Well, you know that saying, when you check off all the possible suspects, what is left is the probable criminal. But," Neil continued, "about fifteen years ago, Steven's brother had a problem with the Mexico cartel, and they were all killed, with no one left to tell what had happened. The file was closed."

"You know a lot about these guys. How come?" asked George.

"I was the detective on the case," Neil responded.

"Did you suspect the brother?" George asked.

"Yes, he killed them, but it was self-defense. He was a war hero. He had a carry permit. It appeared that the cartel wanted him dead. The guys he killed had arrest records a mile long, no convictions but a lot of suspicions. Those guys were somehow connected to the drug cartel. In the end, the DA and everyone involved agreed it was self-defense and closed the case. After that, the cartel was out of business. Do I think he was the drug dealer? No. But someone picked up the business, but whoever it was, he or she was like a ghost. We couldn't find him or her anywhere."

"One-word answer. Yes or no?" George demanded.

"Okay, no. He was a careful insurance executive. The department ruled it self-defense, not a murder," Neil answered.

Just then, George heard Olivia calling him, "George, George, do you want lunch?"

"One second, Neil...yes, honey, I'll have lunch with you. Neil, I have to go, but let's talk again soon." George hung up the phone and went up to join Olivia for lunch.

CHAPTER 20

Maryann walked back into the house, and Melvin responded to her, "Welcome back, Maryann. We got a response from Steven."

"Oh, good," Maryann responded. "But before you read me his answer, what is the status of going dark?"

Melvin responded, "The first two are finished, and the third—the dark web—should be done tonight."

"Okay, Melvin, read me Steven's answer."

"Okay, Maryann, his response was, 'You are in good hands. Keep a low profile. Careful words will get you to the next day.' I suspect these eighteen words from Steven mean more than they say."

"Possibly, but right now it isn't important," Maryann told Melvin and then asked, "Was there any activity while I was gone?"

"No, Maryann," Melvin responded. "The only activity was our regular postman delivering the mail."

"Is the mail still in the mailbox?" Maryann asked.

"Yes," responded Melvin.

"Okay, scan the mail for listening devices and do it every day once the mail is put in my mailbox."

"Yes, I will add it to the daily checklist," Melvin replied. "And there are no listening devices in today's mail."

"Okay, great. Good night, Melvin. It has been a long day."

"Warren, I sent a message back to Maryann: 'You're in good hands, and careful words will get you through to the next day.' Any other thoughts?" asked Steven.

"No," Warren replied. He then asked, "Have you reached out to any of your contacts as to what is going on?"

"No," said Steven. "All my contacts are out of the country on assignment. But I have an idea on how we can contact Maryann and find out what's going on in person."

"What? How?" asked Warren.

Steven continued, "The security system is due for an inspection by Black Ops. The upgrades are usually done online, but we could ask Black Ops to send an individual to meet with Maryann and give her an encoded iPad so we could speak to her."

"Great idea. Call James to ask him if he could arrange it. I would prefer he personally does it. He looks the part," Warren said.

"Warren," Steven said, "you know the only one who could ask and get it done is *you*, so if you want James to do it, *you* must ask him."

"Okay, I'll call James now," Warren answered.

"Hello, James, this is Warren, and I need a favor." Warren walked out to the pool as he talked with James. A couple minutes later, Warren walked back into the living room.

"Well, will he do it?" Steven asked.

Warren smiled. "Of course," he said, "but we had to get Hopscotch Air to give him a round-trip flight. All done. He leaves tomorrow night."

"See? I knew James wouldn't say no to you," Steven said.

"Steven," Warren asked, "can you follow up with Black Ops on the Eagle's Nest property to see if we are any closer to completion?"

Steven looked at his watch and said, "I'll call tomorrow. They have closed already."

Steven and Warren decided to see James off for his trip to visit Maryann, so they headed for the airport.

"James," Warren said, "Maryann is a special person to us. Please take care of her and give her this iPad so she can talk to us."

"Will do," answered James, and he gave Warren and Steven a thumbs-up sign as he climbed into the aircraft.

Hours later, James arrived at Maryann's home in New York. James knocked on the door then stepped back and said, "Warren and Steven sent me."

Maryann asked Melvin, "Can you identify him?"

"Yes, Maryann. It is James from Black Ops, and I just received a text from Steven through the DOD computer that confirms he is James, and Steven and Warren have sent him."

Maryann opened the door and said to James, "It is good to see a friendly face. How are Warren and Steven doing?"

"Very good," answered James. "But can I come in? I have a present for you."

"Oh, yes, excuse me. Come in." James walked into the house and waited for the door to close. "I wasn't sure if we were being watched. Here is your present. It's an encoded iPad that you can use to communicate with Steven or Warren."

Maryann ripped off the gift paper, turned it on, and said, "How do I speak to them?"

James answered, "See the icon labeled steveview? That is the encryption that Steven developed for Skype for the dark web. Hit the icon and it will call them directly." Maryann tapped the icon.

"Hi, Maryann. Is your creep detector operational?" Steven asked with a laugh.

"It's good to hear your voice, but why can't I see you?" Maryann asked.

"Ask Melvin to turn on the video," Steven instructed.

"Melvin," Maryann called.

"Yes, Maryann, I heard Steven's request. Do you want me to turn on the video?" asked Melvin.

"Yes, immediately!" Maryann shouted excitedly.

"Oh, aren't you a sight for sore eyes! Where's Warren?" asked Maryann.

"Thanks for the compliment. Warren is handling an issue down here but should be here shortly. He was the one who wanted to give you the iPad. So update me. Oh, Warren just walked in. Warren, Maryann's on the iPad."

"Oh, hi, Maryann," Warren called out. "How are things up there?" Steven walked over to meet Warren on the sofa so Maryann could see both of them. It was Warren's first look at Maryann since they had left New York.

Warren started, "Okay, give me the lay of the land from beginning to end. Don't leave out anything."

"Okay," Maryann replied. "You were right—the city business is gone. MS-13 lost it to a drug-selling mob from China, but their drugs have lead in them, and they are killing their own customers. The city cops are on a tear trying to find the drug ring that is causing all these ODs. They are starting to come across the border, into Nassau, west of the Meadowbrook Parkway. Fights and killing are an almost weekly event between the MS-13 and the Chinese. It is starting to spook the Nassau cops in that area."

"And in your area?" Warren asked.

"No problems yet," Maryann answered. "But I'm following your suggestions—low profile, and my junior-level associates do all the deals. I gave them a larger cut to keep my face and name out of that business."

"And the volume?" Warren asked.

"Diaz seems to be happy with the volume. It is steady, not down, not up," Maryann replied.

"Are you sure Diaz is happy?" asked Warren.

"Yes, I think I can read him, and with all the problems he has with the Chinese and MS-13 wars, he is happy my business is the same. I guess my business is enough to pay his bills."

They all laughed.

"Okay," said Warren, "what about the elephant in the room—Caroline's death?"

"Yeah," replied Maryann. "Didn't Steven update you?"

"Yes, he did, but I'd rather hear it directly from you," Warren shot back.

"Well, a couple days ago, I had a visit from Nassau County Detective King and this other guy, who did not identify himself. They were here to ask me questions about Caroline's death. But I threw them out before they could ask me anything. The other guy gave me the creeps. But the security system caught their conversation while they were in their car. The creepy guy is an FBI agent. And the very next day, when I check my iPad's Wi-Fi access, there was a Wi-Fi connection labeled FBI SURVEILLANCE TRUCK. Once

I saw that, I shut off all electronic devices and directed Melvin to encrypt everything. He suggested cleaning everything up and only communicating on the dark web and basically going dark. Melvin was able to get the message to you through the back channels of the DOD system. I also purchased two prepaid cell phones to communicate in case of emergencies."

"Tell me more about the Chinese," Warren said, listening intently to Maryann's report.

"They took Chinatown and Flushing and slowly started to gain a small foothold in all the boroughs in the city. MS-13 began taking them on in their usual way and lost. Suddenly, the Chinese foothold became the entire city, and now MS-13 only has a foothold. And behind closed doors, the mayor and governor are talking about legalizing pot. Warren," Maryann continued, "it seems you got out at the right time."

"MS-13 is probably plotting to come after your business," Warren warned.

"Probably," Maryann replied.

"Well, then you need to make a move before MS-13 does. Figure out what the business is worth and sell it to Diaz. He will probably want to keep your people in place," Warren instructed.

"Well, I would take 50 million. The problem is getting a clean check," Maryann said.

"Not really," said Warren quietly.

"What do you mean?" demanded Maryann.

"Art selling," responded Warren.

"Yeah, right. Where would I get art that's worth $50 million that would pass the IRS smell test?" Maryann asked.

Warren and Steven laughed.

"Okay, what's up with you two?" Maryann asked.

"You do," said Steven. "The paintings are on your walls."

"What?" asked Maryann excitedly. "Tell me more."

Steven answered, "The painting in the dining room—the two palm trees with the hammock—legitimately sold for $60 million. And you have eleven other paintings by the same artist. However, his cloud painting only sold for 50 million."

Warren interrupted and said, "And I'm sure the art dealer in Mexico will sell the painting for 50 million, or he'll screw it up and auction it off for 60 million, so you come home without the painting but $54 million richer. Can you think of what you can buy with $30 million?"

"Why 30 million?" asked Maryann.

"Uncle Sam and Uncle Andrew want their cut," replied Warren.

"Okay, wow, that's a lot of taxes," answered Maryann. "Okay, I have a question: how often can we use this iPad to communicate?"

Steven replied, "Technically anytime, but we should be smart about this. If you need to chat, ask Melvin to send a back-channel text. He will know what to do. I'll get the text and then schedule a time to speak, okay?"

"Fine," said Maryann. "I'll text you when I need to talk."

"And if we need to speak with you, I'll text Melvin," Steven said.

"Okay, guys, I better get to bed. It was great to hear your voices and see your faces! Good night."

"Okay, good night," Steven replied.

"Good night, Maryann. Remember what I said about Diaz and MS-13. Be smart and stay safe," said Warren.

CHAPTER 21

The next day at 10:00 a.m., Maryann decided to go for a jog to relieve the stress. As she was on her way back to the house, Melvin alerted her on her Apple Watch of a suspicious car that drove past the house a couple times and was now behind her.

"Melvin, can you run the license plate?" asked Maryann.

"Yes, I will do it immediately," replied Melvin. "Oh, this is a problem. The car is registered to the Chinese Embassy. I strongly suggest you enter the house through the garage, but you better act quickly. They are right behind you,"

Maryann started to sprint toward the garage door. As she reached the driveway, the garage door opened and closed without allowing the individuals in the Chinese Embassy car the ability to capture her.

Shortly thereafter, Melvin explained to Maryann that the people in the embassy car were walking up the front path.

"What?" Maryann continued, "Are they armed?"

"No, they are not armed," replied Melvin. Maryann ran to the computer screen in the kitchen. She saw two Asian males in suits, medium height and medium built, walking toward the front door.

"Melvin, can you detect if they have any weapons?" Maryann asked.

Melvin replied, "No, they do not have any weapons."

"Okay, stand down but constantly sweep the perimeter while I find out what these guys want. I don't want any surprises."

The doorbell rang, and Maryann slowly walked to the door.

"Good morning. My name is Chen, and my partner is Liu. May we come in?"

"No," Maryann replied. "I don't know you, and why would I want to speak with you inside my home?"

"Maryann," Chen replied, "we are in the same business and would like to discuss a joint venture."

"What type of business are you talking about? I own 7-Elevens and real estate."

Liu laughed and said, "We are competitors of Diaz. You may have heard we own New York City."

Then Chen said, "I don't think you want us to discuss our business options in front of the FBI surveillance truck down the street. May we come in now?" Maryann moved out of the way and let them in and showed them to the living room.

"We are not here to give you a problem but to offer you some options," said Chen.

"Options for what?" Maryann asked.

"We know that you have an agreement with the cartel, from Meadowbrook Parkway to the end of the island, or at least to the Brentwood area, south to Heckscher State Park, and we would like to buy that contract from you."

"You said you had options, meaning more than one," Maryann shot back with an attitude.

"Correct," Liu said. "Option two would be to buy your drugs from us, and we would offer you protection from any problems."

Maryann asked, "Do you have a sample of your product?"

"Yes," said Liu, and he reached slowly into his jacket pocket and took out a baggie of white power and some tablets.

Maryann said, "Give them to me. I need to test them before I would consider placing an order with you." Maryann took the baggie and walked into the kitchen. Liu and Chen followed her. She took out a syringe from the drawer and injected a clear fluid into the bag. In seconds, the powder and tablets in the bag turned rust-colored. Maryann turned to them and said, "Your drugs have lead in them. I can't sell this to my clients. If they don't OD, they will certainly die of lead poisoning. I'm not going to jail for the rest of my life for lead poisoning. Sorry, option two is off the table. What are you willing to pay for my contract?"

"For all your inventory and the contract, 65 million, wired to an account of your choosing," replied Liu.

"What about my people?" Maryann asked.

"If they want to join us and follow our way, they can continue, but honestly we have our own personnel," replied Chen.

"Can the money be paid in any manner that I request?" asked Maryann.

"Yes," Chen quickly replied, almost as if he sensed a quick deal could be made. Chen continued, "We can pay you in real estate, art, bank debt, or any currency you desire."

"Will I have to stick around after I commit to this agreement?" Maryann asked.

Chen replied, "It is not necessary, and since we have our own personnel, it won't be required. We strongly suggest you take the money and enjoy the rest of your life away from this territory."

"Okay, let me get this straight. *If* I agree to this, you will pay me in a single payment of $65 million in any mode I request. And once this agreement is made, I have no responsibility to hang around. And I can take my money and go anywhere I want and never be bothered by anyone in your organization. I'm free and clear."

"Yes, you understood our concept," Chen replied.

"One question, how are you going to penetrate the area if your personnel don't know my clients and the neighborhoods?"

Chen replied, "Google, Facebook, and medical records. We have access—"

Liu abruptly interrupted Chen and spoke to him in Chinese. Maryann only could understand a couple words: *too much information* and *don't tell her.*

"So you break into the websites and databases to get info on everyone in the area who uses drugs, legally or illegally, and you approach them like Amazon or Google would to sell your products."

"Something like that," Chen said. "And that's why you should sell to us. Because eventually we will own the area anyway. But we would like to do it peacefully."

"You need to give me forty-eight to seventy-two hours to make a decision," Maryann stated. "And now I suggest you leave my home. I have a lot of thinking to do."

Chen replied, "If you have any questions, you can reach us at this number." He pulled a card from his pocket and started to hand it to Maryann. She saw that it was a Chinese Embassy business card, with the gold-and-red Chinese national emblem. Chen quickly pulled back the card and pulled out another card with just a phone number.

Maryann moved to the door, opened it, and motioned for them to leave. Both left and thanked her for her time. Maryann said nothing and closed the door. Melvin started recording from the external microphones. Liu was speaking to Chen in Chinese. From the tone of his voice, he was upset. Melvin told Maryann, "I'll have the full translation in a few minutes."

Maryann waited on the couch for Melvin's translation.

"Oh, this isn't good," Melvin said.

"What did Liu say?" asked Maryann.

"Liu told Chen in an angry tone, 'You gave her too much information. She doesn't need to know how we do our business or how we get our clients. That is a state secret.' Then Chen replied, 'Don't worry. Dead drug dealers won't tell any state secrets, and then we are $65 million richer.' Liu called Chen crazy and said, 'I'm not touching that money, and if you touch it, I'm reporting you to the ambassador.' Chen called Liu a wimp, and that was the end of their conservation."

"Oh shit, I knew there were more strings attached," Maryann said. "Melvin, text Steven and send him this conversation encoded."

"Maryann," Melvin interrupted, "another car just pulled up, and a guy in a military uniform just got out and is heading for the front door."

"Is he armed?" asked Maryann.

"No," Melvin answered. "He only has a suitcase, and based on the brass on his shoulders, I think he is an admiral."

Suddenly he was knocking on the front door. Maryann thought his knocks sounded really urgent, like he was in a hurry. Maryann opened the door and said, "Hi, who are you, and what are you doing at my front door?"

"I am Admiral John Gregory." Maryann saluted him out of force of habit. "At ease, Sergeant." Maryann was surprised that he knew her military rank but didn't comment. "Do you have a secure place where we can talk?"

"Yes, the back room." Maryann led the way to the safe room.

Once they reached the safe room, the admiral began, "You just met with two Chinese men from the Ministry of State Security, the MSS."

"No, they are drug dealers," Maryann answered.

"Wrong. They work directly for the MSS," Admiral Gregory corrected.

"Okay, exactly what is the MSS?" Maryann already knew what the MSS was, but this gave her some time to think about her situation and to see how much the admiral knew about her and the situation.

"The MSS is the intelligence and security agency for the government of China. It gathers counterintelligence and foreign intelligence and handles political security. It is like our FBI and CIA rolled into one, with the extra role of keeping all their citizens obeying the rules of the Communist party, but they recently took on another responsibility—selling drugs."

"In other words, not nice people," Maryann stated.

"You got it. Truly not nice people," answered Admiral Gregory. "What did you discuss with them?"

"Well, it was…uh…" Maryann stumbled. She didn't want to reveal what she did for a living.

The admiral interrupted her, "Listen, Maryann, we know what you do for a living. You own a 7-Eleven and real estate, but you make the bulk of your money in drug dealing. I don't care, and honestly, neither will the IRS if you help us. So can you tell me what they discussed with you?"

"They want to buy my business—the drug part," Maryann answered, relieved that she didn't have to come up with a cover story.

"What is the deal?" the admiral asked.

"65 million and I am out, leave town, never to be seen again on Long Island or New York. But there was something wrong with the drugs," Maryann stated.

"What do you mean?" asked the admiral.

"I have a test I do on drugs to find out if they're pure, and their drugs turned rust-colored. Their drugs were contaminated with lead. I told them I couldn't sell their product because it would kill my clients, which is why they offered to buy me out. But what does this have to do with the US military?" Maryann asked.

"The Naval Criminal Investigative Service, NCIS, has been trying to solve fifty-eight drug-related deaths of military personnel, mainly ODs. The same MO that is spilling over into the general population. We have traced the problem to these two guys. What else did you find out?" the admiral asked.

"They told me they have broken into the databases of Google and Facebook and have access to medical records. They supply those people with drugs, legal and illegal," Maryann answered.

"Okay, when are you supposed to get back to them with your decision?" asked the admiral.

"Forty-eight to seventy-two hours," answered Maryann.

"We are going to require your assistance, Sergeant," the admiral stated.

"Admiral, no disrespect, but I'm not in the military. If I agree to help you, I'm going to require something from you," Maryann said in a confident and strong tone.

"Remember, Sergeant, you *were* in the military, and we could force you to cooperate," stated the admiral.

Maryann raised her voice and said, "I am in this mess because the military couldn't find my records! I was homeless, living in my car, because military guys like you ordered the deletion of my secret records from the computer. And once they were deleted, I couldn't get the VA benefits that I earned. Now you want my cooperation? You could force me, but you won't get my cooperation, and you won't get these guys either."

Realizing he wasn't going to get anywhere forcing Maryann to cooperate, the admiral finally asked, "What do you want?"

"A presidential pardon for all my crimes, I never testify in court, and none of my business dealings go public. For this, I will give you my full cooperation on the dealings of MS-13, the cartel, and what I know of these Chinese guys. But I'll need protection until all these guys are put away. Do we have a deal?" Maryann asked.

"Are you sure you can deliver enough information to put these guys away for life?" asked the admiral.

"I have enough information to give them the death penalty," Maryann shot back. The admiral didn't respond, so Maryann continued, "Last time I checked, drug trafficking is a federal capital crime, which is punishable by death."

"The presidential pardon, I don't know if I can get that done. The rest is possible if you give dates, places, and the people involved so we can get third-party confirmation," Gregory answered.

"Well, I guess you need to ask the president. Remember, you have forty-eight hours to get all my demands in writing," Maryann stated, looking directly at him. "I suggest you leave now and get to work on this." Maryann got up and walked the admiral to the door. She stood at the door, waving to the admiral as he left. As she closed the door, Maryann called out to Melvin.

"Melvin, text Steven and Warren with a message: need to speak ASAP."

"Understood and done. Waiting for their response," Melvin responded.

On the way to Republic Airport, Admiral Gregory placed a secure call to the White House. "Mr. Robert Case, please."

"Chief of Staff Case's office, how can I help you?"

"This is Admiral Gregory. Please put me through to Mr. Case, please."

"Right away, Admiral."

"Rob, this is Gregory. I need to see you and the president on three issues: fifty-eight unsolved NCIS murders, the Chinese MSS, and a presidential pardon."

"Admiral Gregory," Case said with a breath of exhaustion, "you know it doesn't work this way."

"Rob," the admiral said, "I have only seventy-two hours max to get information to solve these murders and prevent more, so yes, I realize I'm putting you in a tight spot. I'm trying to save military lives. Can you schedule some time for me with the president?"

"I'll get you ten minutes, but I'm warning you, if you can't engage him in the first five minutes, you are toast! He can see you tomorrow at three p.m., but you may have to fly to Mar-a-Lago. I will let you know. And on a personal side, I'm leaving at the end of the year, and I have already given our boss my notice. Only he knows, but probably next week it will leak out."

"What will you do? You've been in some governmental role since the seventies," Admiral Gregory said.

"Got to go. The boss is calling. See you tomorrow at three p.m. Bye," Case stated.

Several hours later, the iPad that Steven sent Maryann turned on with a Skype call. It was Steven and Warren.

"Guys, I have had a very eventful last couple hours, starting with two guys from the Chinese MSS intelligence service and then an NCIS admiral."

"What the hell happened?" Warren asked in a very concerned tone.

"First, the two guys from the MSS knocked on my door and told me they want to partner with me in my business. I asked them, 'What business do you want to partner in, real estate or the 7-Eleven business?' They laughed, but what concerned me was what they knew about my drug business with Diaz and even the territory agreement Warren negotiated with Diaz. How would they know or find out that I do business with Diaz and the cartel? They gave me two options: buy my drugs through them or they would buy my business for 65 million. So I tested their drugs, and it was laced with lead. I have forty-eight to seventy-two hours to tell them which option I will take. But Melvin overheard them talking on the way to their cars, and they said, 'Dead drug dealers tell no stories.' I'm assuming I'm the dead drug dealer they are talking about. So either option, I'm a dead person."

"And the admiral?" Steven asked.

"He's involved with NCIS. There are fifty-eight unsolved murders of military personnel that are pointing to these guys. The admiral wants my help in putting these two MSS agents and the cartel in jail for life or to get them the death penalty. For my involvement, I asked for a presidential pardon, no testifying, and none of my business dealings ever going public."

"That's some demands!" shouted Steven.

"It gets better. The admiral has forty-eight to seventy-two hours to deliver," Maryann replied. As the words came off her lips, she realized the position she was in. There was no way the president would give her a pardon, let alone get her out of testifying. And any business dealing with the Chinese would eventually mean her death. Chen already said he would kill her, and if she'd switch distributors from the cartel to the Chinese, Diaz would kill her first. "Oh shit, I painted myself into a corner!" Maryann exclaimed. "Warren, I need your advice. What are my real options?"

Warren answered, "You're right. You painted yourself into a corner. First, you need to secure the front door. I'm sure you saw what the FBI did to Paul Manafort's front door, and he was cooperating with the government. You need to call Black Ops and build in measures to give you more protection from anyone. Secondly, you need to make the best deal you can with the admiral. You're right in thinking the Chinese and the cartel would eventually kill you and take your business. Either way, you are not in control. At least with the path to the government, you have some options. Even if you don't get a presidential pardon, you could ask to go into witness protection."

"That looks like it is the only option that can keep me alive," Maryann stated.

"Unfortunately," Warren replied. "But first, call Black Ops about the front door and additional property security then wait to hear from the admiral."

"I'm on it, thanks. Bye." Maryann turned the Skype call off and picked up her burner phone and called Black Ops. "Hello, this is Maryann—"

The person on the other end cut her off, "Hi, Maryann, this is James. Is everything okay? How can we help?"

"I need every entrance to the house resecured so no one can get in unless I authorize them to enter."

"What prompted this call?" asked James.

"How the government entered Paul Manafort's home—one knock at the front door with a metal pole, and they're in—I don't want that to happen to me," Maryann explained.

"How fast do you want this done?" asked James.

"Overnight, if that is possible," responded Maryann.

"Overnight, no, but we can have a crew there in two days and be finished that day," answered James.

"Fine," answered Maryann, "but I'm going to need pictures of who is coming and when they should arrive at my front door."

"Understood," said James. "Anything else?"

"Yes, how about a sign on the front lawn that says 'Warning: This house is armed with deadly protection measures. Trespassing on this property without authorization from the owner will lead to *your* death'?" stated Maryann.

"Wow," said James. "Someone pissed you off, and they aren't going to be allowed to do it a second time."

"Correct," said Maryann. "See you in forty-eight hours. Don't forget the pictures and ETA of your men."

"Okay, goodbye," said James and hung up.

Maryann put the burner phone down when the house phone rang. "Melvin, who is calling on the house phone?"

"I believe it to be Admiral Gregory," Melvin replied.

Maryann picked up the phone. "Hello, Admiral. Do you have any good news for me?"

"I'm supposed to meet with the president tomorrow, but the presidential pardon is a long shot because you haven't been convicted of any federal crime. But I have the DOJ, the DOD, and my staff working on solutions. But I wanted to be straight with you on the presidential pardon. It is probably not in the cards. But I think I understand your situation. Both the Chinese and the cartel are going to want you dead if you testify against them. I assume you're going to want to take all your assets with you wherever you go. So my real question is, are you going to want some type of witness protection program? Or do you want a place like your friend Warren has in Mexico?"

When the admiral mentioned Warren, she immediately thought, *How the hell does he know about Warren?* But she quickly shot back, saying, "No, not exactly, and under no circumstances will I submit a proffer or have any of our discussions taped or transcribed."

"Why not? Where is your attitude coming from?" asked the admiral.

"One of your US attorneys in the Midwest let a woman's proffer agreement go on a public site, and that woman was shot dead within eight hours of the information going public. And that US attorney, a federal employee, was mysteriously out of town on a medical leave for a month."

"Oh," replied the admiral.

"Yeah, all you can say is 'oh'!" Maryann replied. Maryann started to raise her voice. "Where is this coming from? It's the distrust and the lack of integrity of the people in the so-called justice department. Oh, and by the way, how did you know about my friend Warren?"

"Maryann," replied the admiral, "with the NSA intelligence network, we follow *all our friends*. Let me get back to work and prepare for my meeting with the president. I'll call you right after. Bye."

As she hung up, Maryann heard the burner phone ring, signaling a text message. She picked it up and saw that it was from James: "Crew should arrive no later than tomorrow afternoon. But trying to get them there early in a.m. Working on the pics. Will send soon." *Good*, Maryann thought. *Something is finally going right for me.* Then she thought, *Tomorrow is going to be an action-packed day—the admiral will get back to me on the president's decision, and James's security team will be fortifying my home.*

Later that night, James sent pictures of his crew and told her they were in the air and would arrive at her front door at 8:00 a.m. "Melvin," Maryann called out, "I'm sending you the pictures of the crew coming to fortify the entrances to the house. They'll be here around eight in the morning. When they arrive, please check the crew against these pictures. Only let the ones in the pictures onto the property. If there are any problems, alert me, James, Steven, and Warren."

CHAPTER 22

James's Black Ops security crew arrived precisely at 8:00 a.m. "Maryann," Melvin called out, "the crew is here, and they all check out. Shall I let them in?"

"Yes," answered Maryann. She met the security crew at the door.

The leader of the crew came forward to identify himself. "Good morning, Maryann. My name is Chris. James sent us to fortify your home. Do you need to go over anything with me?"

"Do you understand what I want to be accomplished?" asked Maryann.

"Yes, you want your home so secure that no one could enter it the way they entered Paul Manafort's house, and you want a sign on the front lawn stating something to the effect 'Don't piss off the owner. Your life might depend on it.'"

Maryann smiled and said, "Close, but I will give you the exact wording later."

"Good," responded Chris.

As Maryann walked away from Chris, Melvin sent a text alert to her burner phone. It read, "Look at monitor. Detective King is back." As Maryann looked at the monitor from within the safe room, she saw King's car stopped in front of the house. He didn't get out; he just sat and watched the house and all the workers rushing to complete the reconstruction of her home security.

In the afternoon, Chris came to Maryann to tell her that the work was going surprisingly fast and that they should be done by that night.

A little while later, Melvin texted Maryann that Chen was driving by the property. Watching on the monitor from within the safe room, Maryann saw him drive by a second time. She began to feel the outside world closing in on her. *I thought I had another day with that SOB.* Then she remembered what Warren had said about Chen and Diaz wanting her business. Then she thought, *If I could get them fighting with each other, I could buy some time.* Just then, Chris came to speak with her. "Not now, Chris. I must make a phone call. Can we talk later?" Maryann asked him. Chris nodded his head, and as he walked away, Maryann placed her call.

"Hello, Mr. Diaz, this is Maryann. We have a problem, and I was hoping you could take the problem off my hands."

"I'm listening. What is your problem?" Diaz asked.

"Two Chinese MSS agents, named Chen and Liu, came to see me yesterday."

Diaz interrupted, "What did they want?"

"Diaz," Maryann answered, "what do you think they wanted? *Our* business. They are somehow linked into the medical databases, so their cover is legal medication. Then they convert their customers to a higher-profit medication for them and a smaller co-payment for the clients. Eventually, the whole community is hooked and dealing with them. We need Chen to disappear—he's the hothead of the two. He is also the one who is gunning for *us.*"

"Me too?" Diaz questioned.

"Yes," Maryann responded. "They know a lot about you. They were telling me who your associates are, where you live, your family, and that they, MSS, don't mind losing a few battles or soldiers because they always plan long-term. And their long-term goal is to win the drug war. They want to be king. It's like they're refighting the opium wars to enslave the West to the drug the way the British did it to China in the 1800s, which resulted in widespread addiction in China."

"TMI," Diaz replied. "I don't want a history lesson. I just need to know where I can find Chen."

Maryann responded, "I will call him to meet me at the store at three a.m. Do you remember the grassy lot on the side of the building?"

"Yes," said Diaz.

"You can handle our problem there because it doesn't have cameras. But you have to take care of him close to the building behind the shed. That way, no one will be able to see anything from the street.

So, Diaz," Maryann continued, "I need you at the store around midnight, just in case he comes early."

"Okay," said Diaz.

"See you then." Maryann hung the phone up. The next phone call she made on the burner phone was to Chen.

"Chen, do you know who this is?" Maryann asked.

Chen answered, "Yes, Mar—"

"No names," Maryann interrupted before he could finish her name.

"Okay," Chen said, and then he continued, saying, "I'm surprised you called."

"Really," Maryann said sarcastically. "Listen, I have questions, so we need to meet. Tonight at my 7-Eleven store at three a.m. And before you start asking why at three a.m., it is because no one is around at that time and only one employee is working the cash register. You can bring Liu if you want, but I got the feeling that you are the person calling the shots and Liu is along for the ride. So can you make it at three?"

"Yes, and I will bring Liu," Chen answered.

"Fine," Maryann responded. Maryann texted Diaz: "We are on for the breakfast mtg, but plus one."

As Maryann got off the phone, Chris walked over to her and asked, "Can we talk now?"

"Sure, what's up?" Maryann asked.

"I need your words for the lawn sign," Chris stated.

"Here it is." Maryann handed Chris a piece of paper with her wording for the sign.

Chris read the words out loud: "Warning: This house and property are armed with deadly protection measures. Trespassing on this property without authorization from the owner will lead to *your* death. Any questions, call 516-798-4200."

He stopped reading and looked up at Maryann. "Do you really want to put your number on the sign?" he asked.

"Yes, how else will the kids be able to retrieve their football from my front lawn?" Maryann said.

CHAPTER 23

Before Maryann knew it, it was time to leave for the store and the meeting with Diaz and Chen. She got to the store and made sure everything was set on the side lot: blocked from street views. And at 3:00 a.m., any customers were just getting coffee and getting right back into their cars and leaving.

Diaz showed up on time, and Maryann took him to the side lot. Maryann noticed two cars parked on the side street. "Are they your guys?" she asked Diaz.

"Of course. I want this to go smoothly and quietly," Diaz replied.

"Whatever," Maryann responded as she walked away and back into the store.

Chen and Liu came early. Maryann watched as they pulled into a parking spot and got out of the car. Maryann moved from behind the cash register to the front door. As they walked close to the door, she opened it and walked out. Her heart was racing. She motioned to them to follow her to the side lot.

Chen caught up to her and stated, "Let's meet inside."

"Can't. Cameras are in the store. The side lot has no cameras and no view from the street," Maryann answered.

As they walked onto the side-lot grass, two cars pulled into the 7-Eleven parking lot, directly in front of the shed. There was a lot of laughing, and ten teenage kids came running up the side street. Both Chen and Liu stared at what was going on, and as Liu went for his gun, Diaz came from behind the building and stabbed him in the back. The "kids" pushed Chen up against the shed, and Diaz pulled out a needle and said, "This is my territory."

Maryann tried to leave, but the people from the cars held her to watch Diaz as he jabbed the needle into Chen's eye. Someone covered his mouth, so you barely heard a sound. Someone else came out with two huge garbage bags, and the "kids" tucked Chen and Liu in separate bags and dropped them in the trunks of the cars. Another jumped in Chen's car and drove off.

Diaz turned to Maryann and said, "Problem solved."

"Really?" Maryann answered. "Where are you taking the problems?" Diaz's thugs were still holding on to her. She realized Diaz was sending a message to her: "If you cross me, I will kill you in an excruciating manner."

"Not for you to worry about," Diaz answered.

"Can I go back inside now?" Maryann asked. Diaz nodded his head.

As she left, she realized that Diaz was uncontrollable and no different from MS-13 and that her window of freedom was shrinking. Other people seemed more in control of her life than she was, and she didn't like it and wouldn't allow it to continue.

⁂

Early the next morning, George called Neil. "Hey, Neil, did you see that sign on Maryann's front yard? Is that legal?" asked George.

"Apparently it is," replied Neil. "She visited the seventh precinct early today and told the commanding officer that she has guns and will shoot first and ask questions later. She has been harassed three times by unwanted visitors who entered the home, and the fourth time included Detective King, who brought an unauthorized visitor from the FBI who literally scared the hell out of her. She felt he was casing the house. Detective King confirmed that the FBI agent acted like an asshole. He didn't identify himself and used none of the usual protocol. So they have informed every car in the area to call the commanding officer before entering the property. The commanding officer was very specific: 'Don't step on the property, not even the sidewalk,' until he gives the okay to proceed."

"When did she pull this off?" asked George.

156

"Wait," said Neil, "you haven't heard all of it yet. That was the second time in one day that she visited the seventh precinct. The first was very early in the morning. Do you remember Diaz from the cartel, the guy who seems like nothing sticks to him?"

"Yeah," said George.

"Well, at like five in the morning, Maryann walked into the precinct demanding to see the commanding officer and then told him where to find surveillance footage of Diaz killing two drug dealers."

"Where was the surveillance camera?" asked George.

"Across the street at McCann's Pub. The camera was angled perfectly to see the entire murder. From the bank across the street, they picked up the license plates of the cars that drove away with the two dead drug dealers' bodies. There were about twenty to twenty-three people involved, and thanks to the surveillance, the Nassau and Suffolk County Police Departments are in the process of arresting all of them."

"Wow!" George replied. "So is Maryann the drug dealer who gave the overdose to Caroline?"

"We will never know. Right now, the police are so happy to have Diaz and his MS-13 gang in jail and off the street. It looks like Maryann is untouchable. That footage will lead to more arrests, and some of these guys will turn state's evidence," responded Neil.

"You mean a proffer," stated George.

"Yes," responded Neil, "but the footage should also help in arresting this Chinese gang. Maryann put herself in a great bargaining position. The DAs are going to want her cooperation to put more MS-13 and the Chinese gang in jail, and they gave her immunity. They aren't going to let one overdose victim get in their way of putting all these guys in jail."

"Well, that isn't going to sit well with Jonathan," George stated.

"Yeah, but let me put it another way: putting Diaz away and locking up his crew or deporting them will save thousands of lives and millions of dollars in overtime and give the Nassau and Suffolk PD, the DA, and the feds a whole lot to celebrate," Neil answered.

George answered, "You're right. This way the drug dealers will stop running drugs in Burns Park, for a while at least." They both laughed.

"Well, George, your four-pebble mystery is over. Problem solved."

"Yup. Should be a lot quieter in the neighborhood now. Talk to you soon, Neil."

❦

Later that day, back at home, Maryann got a call from the admiral. "Good afternoon, Maryann, this is Admiral Gregory."

"It is almost evening, Admiral. What can I do for you?" Maryann replied.

"First, I want to thank you for telling the police about the surveillance footage."

Maryann interrupted, "How the hell did you find out about that?"

The admiral replied, "Maryann, it's a very small world. Both the Nassau and Suffolk County PDs called for help with ICE to get these guys deported ASAP. Just to let you know, half of Diaz's crew is already on a military plane and being shipped back to their countries. Diaz and the other half will be held in federal prisons without bail."

"Well, that's good for the community, but what about your conversation with the president and getting me the help I need?" asked Maryann.

The admiral started slowly, "Well...you remember that I told you it was a long shot, right?" He paused.

"Yeah," Maryann answered.

"The president denied you a pardon based on the fact that you haven't been convicted of a crime, but he reminded me about the Defense Secrets Act of 1911 and subsequent laws and regulations, such as the United States government classification system. The president's chief of staff and the president seem to think your case falls right into this act, especially since the MSS is involved and they are a foreign power. The president will issue an executive order classifying all the information regarding you as top secret and for the eyes of only a handful of people—the attorney general, Department of Defense secretary, the chief of NCIS, and the president. What the president

158

and I want is your cooperation regarding any other information you could give us so we can put more of these people behind bars."

"When does this all happen?" asked Maryann.

"My understanding is it was in the works when I left the Oval Office, and I should be receiving a call or a hand-delivered letter from the president any day now."

"Well, when you get it, call me. Good night." Maryann was emotionally exhausted from the day's events. She didn't want to think or talk anymore. She turned off her cell phone and sat for a while in the kitchen just thinking about what had occurred in the last twenty-four hours. Finally, she breathed a sigh of relief. Only one day ago, she had felt like a caught caged animal on the way to the slaughterhouse. Now two of her tormentors were dead, and the federal government imprisoned the other one. Now she thought she just needed to stay ahead of the federal government until she could drop off the grid and disappear. As she started to daydream more, her cell phone rang. It was the admiral calling back.

"Yes, Admiral. What do you want now?" asked Maryann, not hiding how annoyed she was.

"Nothing. I just wanted to tell you the letter was just hand-delivered to me."

"What does it say?" asked Maryann.

"What I told you," answered the admiral. "The classification of top secret, code word *eyes only.*"

"So the information about the proffer was correct. That witness is dead," Maryann stated.

"That case had no effect on the president's decision on your matter," the admiral replied. "Maryann," he continued, "I know that you told me that information so you would get the best deal you could. But that case had no bearing on you or your situation, so when I talked to the president, I did not bring it up. Once we were done with your case, I did tell the president about what happened to the witness who gave the proffer and that I had confirmed the information. He wasn't happy.

"All I can tell you is that the federal prosecutor and his team are under ethical investigation. The president had instructed the attorney general to fire the bastard before the end of the week, put the rest under arrest, and break into their homes the way they broke into Manafort's home. It is time the jailors get the treatment they give to the jailed. His words. By the way, do you know of any other info on MS-13 or Diaz?"

"Yes, but this has to be the last piece of info I can give you for a while," answered Maryann.

"Okay," agreed the admiral.

"Have NCIS comb the bay side of the roadway at East Gilgo. You will find an MS-13 body shot in the head. That was done by Diaz. His prints will be on the bullets from the gun, and you will probably find the gun in the home of one of the guys you arrested for the MSS murders."

"Oh, one other thing," the admiral stated. "All your records have been sealed in NCIS computers and wiped from all other databases. What this means is you are not in the defense computers and will not be eligible for any VA benefits. If people are going to start looking for you, that is the first place they would look. So if you have no footprint there, it will just make it more difficult for them to find you."

Maryann began to laugh. "You may remember this all started because you couldn't find my military service records. You now found them and wiped them out. I guess I owe you a thank-you." Maryann continued, "So does this mean I'm not going to hear from you anymore? Are we done?"

"No," the admiral said quickly. "I have over fifty-eight deaths of military people to investigate and solve. Hopefully, you can aid in solving those deaths."

"Admiral," Maryann answered, "I told you I only met those guys once. As I told you before, those guys have access to medical databases, and they sell drugs, legally and illegally, to the same people. I guess when the patient or user can't get any more prescription renewals of the drugs, they, MSS, illegally sell them a 'generic replacement.' The user probably doesn't even know what they are getting. They are poisoned by the same people who deliver their doctor's prescribed drugs. That's why their business is growing so fast and with no force. They are supplying everyone and taking over territories without firing one shot. If I were you, I'd check each death against the medication prescribed by a doctor that eventually changed to less expensive drugs. The person stops the medication and starts using street drugs supplied by MSS."

"How did they get into the medical databases?" asked the admiral.

"They hacked them," Maryann said. "Isn't that what the Red Chinese are experts at doing? Or they are part of the insurance network that supplies the drugs. Listen, thank you for the info about the president's letter, but it's late, and I have to get some sleep. I have no further info. So good night, Admiral." Maryann turned off her cell phone again and walked into her bedroom and quickly fell asleep.

Chapter 24

Maryann's much-needed sleep was suddenly interrupted at 3:00 a.m. by a loud alarm, flashing lights, and Melvin shouting, "Maryann, wake up! We are about to be invaded. I am armed and seek direction as to what actions you want to be taken." Maryann quickly jumped out of bed and ran into the safe room. She viewed the monitor to see what was going on outside. It was still dark out, but with the infrared cameras, she could see all the movements by the individuals and could hear what was being said. She could see that the individuals had FBI markings on their uniforms.

She started to get angry and thought, *After all the info I gave the cops and the admiral, they are coming to arrest me in the middle of the night. Great.*

"Melvin," Maryann said, "seal all outside doors, seal the safe room, and transfer all information on the garage security system to the system in the safe room. Wipe the garage system clean." Before Maryann could finish her direction, Melvin and all the monitors went dark; someone cut the electricity to the house. Maryann's body began to shake in panic and fear. Steven didn't prepare her for this; Melvin was gone. She thought how she was going to protect herself. She grabbed the gun she stored in the safe room and checked if the windows and doors were sealed; they were. As she took a deep breath and began to think about a plan B, Melvin came back on.

"Maryann, Maryann!" Melvin shouted.

"What happened to you? Where did you go?" Maryann asked in a nervous tone.

"They cut the power, but the battery backup powered me back on," said Melvin.

"Good." Maryann continued, "Turn the garage system off and disconnect it from the network. Set the garage system to self-destruct if anyone tries to access the info without the correct access code."

"There are men on the lawn. What actions do you wish me to take against them?" Melvin asked.

Maryann answered quickly, "Take them out—aim at their knee-caps!" As the word *caps* came out of Maryann's mouth, she heard the shots ring out and watched on the monitor as the FBI agents went down. Blood was all over her front lawn, and by the faces of the agents, Maryann could tell they were in terrible pain. Maryann was both sympathetic and pissed in the same emotion. As the shots rang out, Maryann's neighbors started turning on their lights to see what was going on, and a dozen 911 calls were made.

One FBI agent had made it to the front door and was trying to break down the door with a battering ram. After the third or fourth try, he hurled the device through the glass window and tried to climb through the opening. A couple of the neighbors started shooting at the intruders; one had a bullhorn and was ordering them to lay down their guns and surrender. One voice yelled back, "We are the FBI. Stop shooting at us!"

On the monitor, Maryann was able to see the face of the person yelling to the neighbors. It was that creepy agent who had come to the house with Detective King. Maryann and the entire neighborhood could hear police sirens coming from all directions. Finally, the first Nassau County-sector car arrived and went to the house of the neighbor with the bullhorn.

The patrol cop, with his gun drawn, asked the neighbor, "What the hell is going on here?"

The neighbor said, "We think these guys are trying to break into the house next door. They stated they are FBI, but what the hell is the FBI doing in a neighborhood at three a.m., shooting up a residential house? They look more like drug dealers."

The cop took the bullhorn, identified himself, and told the FBI to lay down their guns and get on the ground facedown with their hands on their necks.

The FBI agent answered, "We are the FBI, and we are here to arrest the owner of this house."

The cop answered back, "I don't care if you are the president. You will cease and desist immediately, or there will be extreme action taken against you." Just then, the tactical command center pulled up in front of the house where the cop was. By the time it came to a complete stop, fifty cops in full combat gear had exited the vehicle, ready to engage the enemy.

Maryann, who was still watching on the monitor in the safe room, saw that the FBI agent who had thrown the ramming bar against the window still wasn't able to get into the house. She overheard him talking to his supervisor, telling him that he couldn't get into the house because there were gates in front of every window. He said he had walked around the house and it didn't look like there was anyone inside the house. The supervisor told him about the problems outside and ordered him to assist his fellow agents who were injured.

Out of the twenty agents who came to arrest Maryann, there were fifteen wounded, and five were in Nassau County Police handcuffs.

The commander of the tactical unit asked one of his officers to get the agent in charge into the command vehicle ASAP.

A few minutes later, the officers arrived at the command center with the FBI agent in charge.

"Here he is, Chief," said the officer. "His name is Special Agent Wiley."

"Oh shit, Wiley, you're that FBI asshole agent who gave the woman who lives in this house the creeps! Excellent. What's next?"

"Hold on. I have a warrant for that woman's arrest," said Agent Wiley.

"Really?" said the tactical commander. "Then why didn't you follow FBI protocol by notifying the local police department to assist you with this arrest warrant?"

Wiley didn't answer.

The commander asked, "Do you even have an arrest warrant?"

Wiley answered, "Yes, it is in my pocket. Uncuff me, and I'll get it for you."

"No, thanks," the commander said as he reached into Wiley's suit-jacket pocket. He found the warrant and read the paperwork. He yelled out, "This warrant isn't signed!" The commander got close to Wiley's face and said, "You are going to jail for a long time, and my department is sending your friends in Washington a bill for our time and expense." The commander turned to the officer and said, "Get this criminal out of here and bring him to the county jail." The commander watched as the officer put Wiley in the patrol car. When he was in, the commander motioned to the officer to come over to him. The commander turned his back to the patrol car and leaned into the officer and said quietly, "This makes no sense. Something else is at play here. Watch your six."

After the patrol car left, with Agent Wiley sitting in the back looking dejected, the commander turned to the officers standing there and said, "Let's clean this place up and go home. I think this neighborhood has had enough excitement for one night." Twenty minutes later, all the cop cars and the command center had left.

Maryann was still in the safe room watching the monitors as the cops outside were cleaning up. She dialed the admiral's number on her burner phone. "Maryann, I didn't expect to hear from you. Is there a problem?" asked the admiral.

"Yes," answered Maryann. "I just had twenty FBI agents in front my house, and they were saying they have an arrest warrant for me. What is going on?"

"Who is the FBI agent in charge?"

"I believe it to be Wiley," answered Maryann.

"Do you have a safe place to stay?" asked the admiral.

"Yes," replied Maryann, "but the Nassau County Police have arrested your Agent Wiley for not having the arrest warrant signed and not informing local law enforcement of the FBI's intent."

"While you were talking," the admiral stated, "I checked the justice department database. There is no warrant out for you. Let me check his cell phone. He got a call last night about nine o'clock from one of the MSS cell phone numbers we've been tracking. At ten p.m., he texted them, 'All set 3:00 a.m. See you afterward.' It looks like the

CHAPTER 25

After lying awake for another hour, too wired and worried to sleep, the exhaustion finally took over, and Maryann fell into a deep sleep. She was jolted awake in the late morning by her phone ringing. "Maryann, its Admiral Gregory. I have bad news. Wiley is dead. When my staff arrived at the Nassau County jail, they found him dead in his cell. They are doing an autopsy, but my staff is convinced that Wiley's death is the same MO as the open cases at NCIS, which means all these deaths were the work of MSS. You are obviously in danger. You need to go to a place where you are totally protected. Maryann, I have a plane at Republic. It will fly you anywhere. Get whatever you need—just essentials—and get to the airport as quickly as possible."

"Thank you. I'll be there in an hour," said Maryann. She hung up and called Steven. With every ring that he didn't pick up, her anxiety jumped another level. Finally, he answered.

"Maryann, hi. What is going on?" asked Steven.

"I need your help. It is way too hot here. I need a place to lie low for a while. Can you and Warren help?" asked Maryann.

"Is this a secure line?" asked Steven.

"Yes," answered Maryann, "but can you help me?" Steven could tell Maryann was at the end of her rope.

"Who are you hiding from?" asked Warren. "The feds, the cartel?"

"Neither. I'm hiding from the MSS. I made a deal with the feds. They are helping me get out of here. The cartel and MS-13 are all in jail for killing two MSS agents. Can I hide out with you?" Maryann's voice showed her anxiety.

"Yes, of course," Warren answered quickly. "Your pilot will need these coordinates to reach our airfield. Write them down. The coordinates are 21 degrees south, 2 minutes, and 12 seconds by 86 degrees north, 52 minutes, 37 seconds. Maryann, tell the pilot this is a private airport. Your plane will be pulled into a hangar where armed guards will meet you."

"Okay, got it," said Maryann.

"When will you arrive?" Warren asked.

"I'm not sure, but I will be leaving in an hour from Republic," said Maryann. "But I need to gather my stuff and get going. Bye." Maryann took three large suitcases from the closet and thought, *Clothes, cash, and paintings*. Maryann went to her closet, collected everything that would work in Mexico's climate, and threw it all into one suitcase. She took a second suitcase into the tunnel to the cash room and stuffed that suitcase with the largest bills she could find. With that done, she headed back to the house, where she thought, *How do I get ten paintings worth 40 million apiece in a suitcase?* That was when she remembered she had an art tube with an over-the-shoulder strap. She took the canvases off the wooden frames and rolled them into the tube. Almost ready to go, Maryann walked back into the safe room and saw the security cameras and the system were still on high alert.

Melvin, at that moment, asked, "Where are you going, Maryann, and what should I do?"

Maryann replied, "Protect the house and the garage. Don't let anyone enter the house and keep the safe-room door locked, slide the metal covers down on all the windows, and when I leave, lock all the outer doors. I don't know when I will be back, but I *will* be back. So, Melvin, you are in charge. Protect my home. I will have access to you remotely using the code word *almostgone2019*."

Maryann dragged the two suitcases and the art tube into the garage, where her Range Rover, already started by Melvin, was waiting. She quickly threw the cases and art into the car. As the garage door rose, Maryann called out to Melvin and said, "It's been fun. Now lock it all down. See you soon."

As she pulled out of the driveway, the admiral called her cell phone. "Are you on your way?" he asked. She sensed some urgency in his voice.

"Yes, I'm in the car, driving toward the airport as we speak," answered Maryann.

"What is your ETA?" asked the admiral.

"Is there a problem?" asked Maryann.

"Yes, MSS field agents have been spotted on 135 heading south and another on Route 110 heading north to the airport. Take the back road by the cemetery. The plane is fueled and ready to go as soon as you get there, so hurry. I want you in the air ASAP. And don't hang up. Keep me on speaker," ordered Admiral Gregory.

"Copy that," replied Maryann.

"Maryann," said the admiral. "MSS has just turned onto the block by the cemetery, they are headed right for you!"

"How far away are they" Maryann asked

"Less than a mile and closing" answered the admiral

"Okay, what's the plan?" asked Maryann.

"In five hundred feet," said the admiral "there is a gate that leads right onto the runway if you hit it straight on you will break open the gate and be moments away from my plane. hit it hard!"

"Got it" interrupted MaryAnn loudly. Maryann floored the Range Rover, it hit the gates head on and knocked the gate off its hinges. Maryann smiled to herself happy to be insider a range rover which is built like a civilian tank.

"I'm on the runway" screamed out MaryAnn.

"Maryann hurry MSS is right behind you" answered the admiral

"Shit! They're shooting at me. I'm on the runway, and I see the plane. My windshield just shattered!"

"She's under attack! Give her cover!" yelled the admiral, on another phone, to the officers on the plane. Two men came out of the plane and returned fire, giving Maryann enough time to get onto the plane with her luggage and art tube.

Just as the plane was speeding down the runway, the Range Rover that was filed with bullet holes exploded. As the car burned, two Suffolk County patrol cars arrived, and the police officers took control of the situation. By the time the plane was in the air, the MSS field agents were in handcuffs.

The pilot called Admiral Gregory and said, "All cargo aboard. No damages."

"Good work, gentlemen. Thanks," replied the admiral.

As they reached cruising altitude, a TV screen rose from the cabinet and turned on. That's when Maryann noticed she was the only one on the plane besides the crew. Her attention turned back to the TV when she heard a voice coming from it. "Hi Maryann," said Admiral Gregory.

"I thought there was going to be some of your people on this plane," Maryann replied.

"No, there's been a change in plans, but first I need your destination coordinates."

"Okay, here they are." Maryann read the coordinates that Warren had told her from the scrap of paper in her pocket. "And why has the plan changed?" asked Maryann.

"The MSS has put a hit out on you. They believe you had their men killed. We are trying to remove it diplomatically, but I think a bunch of arrests like the ones at the airport and of the rest of the MSS guys who are dealing drugs will calm them down and prove to them the error of their ways. But in the meantime, you must stay out of sight. Do you have any questions for me?" asked the admiral.

"How did Wiley find me if you wiped me out of the system?" asked Maryann.

"He didn't see you in the system. I know that because we checked every computer he had access to. He never accessed your records. He probably just remembered you from when Detective King and he made that unannounced visit to your home. I wish you a safe and speedy trip. Contact me when you can. Bye."

With that, the TV went black and back down into the cabinet. The crew cabin door opened, and one of them shouted, "Relax! We will be at your destination in four and a half hours. If you need anything, just knock on the door and feel free to help yourself to the fridge. It has both food and drinks in it."

Halfway into the flight, the copilot opened the door and walked back to the fridge to get a sandwich and something to drink. Maryann asked, "Can you tell me who you work for?"

"Sure. The NCIS," the copilot replied.

"Then what exactly are your orders?" Maryann asked.

"Precisely as the admiral said. Fly you wherever you want to go, get you there safely and securely, and then fly home to DC." He turned to walk back into the cockpit but stopped and turned back to Maryann and said, "I realize you are nervous about this move, but we are the personal flight crew for the admiral. He wants you to reach your destination safely and, if need be, anywhere else. So please sit back and relax." He smiled and turned to enter the cockpit.

A couple hours later, the cockpit door opened, and the copilot looked back at Maryann and said, "In twenty minutes, we will be landing. Fasten your seat belt. We understand this is a short runway." As they touched down and were taxiing to the airport hangar, a million things ran through Maryann's mind. How would Warren and Steven greet her? She looked into the mirror to make sure she was presentable for whatever she was landing into. Her thoughts were interrupted by the copilot. "Maryann, the admiral wanted me to read this to you when we landed: 'The past is gone. You only have today. Grab it, hold on to it, live for each moment, think of tomorrow, use your talents today to improve your tomorrows.'"

When he finished, he handed Maryann the note. It said, "For safekeeping." The copilot then said, "It is my understanding that the crew must exit first then you." Maryann looked out of the window and was relieved to see the smiling faces of Warren and Steven. She studied their faces to try to read them. Were they really happy to see her or just being polite or taking care of their liability? Maryann thought, *Where is that sixth sense that God gave women?* As she wondered, she noticed the joy on Warren's face, and she could tell it was genuine. Her anxiety disappeared, and she finally felt relaxed and let out a long deep breath.

As she was just about to sit back down, a soldier entered the cabin and told her she must deplane now. When she went to pick up her bags, the soldier told her to leave them and said, "Right now, all we need is you and your papers. Your belongings will come later."

As Maryann walked toward the security checkpoint, the chief security officer greeted her with a smile and said, "Maryann, I assume. Mr. Warren has told us to expect you." As she reached for her passport, he said, "It isn't necessary. Mr. Warren has supplied all the info that the security department needs."

"What about my luggage?" Maryann asked.

"They are taking your luggage off now and delivering it to Mr. Warren's car," replied the security officer. "You have a good night now." As Maryann walked through the gate, Warren and Steven were there to greet her.

Steven gave her a big hug and a polite kiss on the cheek; Warren put his hands on Maryann's shoulders and looked directly into her eyes and smiled. He let his hands slide down her arms until he was holding her hands in his and said quietly, "Welcome home," and hugged her. As they turned and walked toward the car, he held her hand again. As they got closer to the vehicle, Warren suddenly but gently let go of her hand as if he hadn't noticed he was holding it and then used his other hand to open the car door for her.

As Maryann got into the car, she wondered, *Why did he pull away? Where is that sixth sense when I need it?* Warren started the car and then turned around to look at Maryann. He just smiled and then started driving. His smile reduced her anxiety level once again.

During the drive to their house, Steven did all the talking, explaining all the sights. He shared details about whose home was whose and how and why this beautiful community was built. Then Steven turned to Maryann and said, "Do you remember the people who did your security system, Black Ops?"

"Yes," said Maryann, "and they did a great job. The system works flawlessly."

"Well, the same precision they used to build your system was used to create this community," Steven said.

The car slowed down and made a turn onto what looked like a jungle path.

Warren looked in the rearview mirror and sensed that Maryann was concerned. He said, "Our house is at the end of this driveway. We will be there in a few minutes." Suddenly, the big beautiful house appeared out of the jungle.

Once in the house, Steven started to show her around and point out all the amenities. Then Steven said, "Let me show you to your bedroom." Once in the bedroom, Steven continued, "Warren's room is next door. We both agreed this should be your room because it has the best view of the pool. Why don't you wash up and get comfortable?" Just then, Warren walked in, dragging Maryann's luggage.

"What have you got in here?" Warren asked.

"Just what every woman needs—clothes, cash, and millions in painted canvases," answered Maryann.

They all laughed. As Steven and Warren left Maryann's bedroom, the house phone rang. It was the contractor for Eagle's Nest with good news. Warren turned to Steven and told him, "Black Ops said Eagle's Nest is done, and they want us to do a walk-through." Warren turned back to the phone and said, "I need to check my schedule and flight times to see when we can get there. Once I get that together, I will call you back on this number, okay? Got it. Bye." Warren hung up the phone.

"What else did he say?" asked Steven.

"He told me what the total cost was for all the renovations. It was a little over budget, but he said the house is totally wired for off-grid energy production and it is fully furnished. And he reminded me that the property has a landing strip for STOL aircraft. He also thought that would be the best way to see the property."

As they were discussing plans to fly to Idaho to do the walk-through of the updated property, the house phone rang again. This time Steven picked it up.

"Hello? Oh, hi, Uncle John. How did you get this number?" Steven asked.

"You do remember who I work for, right?" answered Uncle John.

"Yes," replied Steven. "NCIS and the federal government."

"Right. Steven, get Warren on the phone. He needs to hear this too."

"Okay," replied Steven. "Warren, Uncle John needs us both on the phone." Warren picked up the phone in the dining room.

"Hi, Uncle John. How is NCIS treating you?" asked Warren.

"Good, but you have a problem on the way. The Chinese MSS has put a hit on your houseguest. My understanding is they are on their way to your location. I would leave immediately," said Uncle John. "I suggest you charter a plane from your airport, get your stuff together, and get the hell out of there. These guys aren't playing around."

"Okay, we will leave within the hour," said Warren and hung up.

Warren told Steven to call James and ask him to charter a plane and inform him about MSS coming to visit.

"Got it," replied Steven.

"I'm going to pack a bag for the two of us for Eagle's Nest," said Warren. "When you get off the phone, tell Maryann we are leaving to see Eagle's Nest immediately."

Steven walked into Warren's bedroom and said, "I just got off the phone with James. He said he would have a plane ready and fueled in twenty-five minutes and not to worry about MSS. His security crew will handle them."

Warren continued to pack their bags. "Don't forget to tell Maryann that we are leaving for Eagle's Nest in twenty-five minutes."

"On it," replied Steven. He went back to Maryann's bedroom, where she had just finished showering and getting on some fresh, clean weather-appropriate clothes.

"Maryann, we have to go check out Eagle's Nest, our property in Idaho, so don't unpack. We will just take all three suitcases," said Steven.

"Is there a problem?" asked Maryann.

"No," replied Steven. "We have been waiting for this call for a while. Part of the contract states that we must do a physical walk-through to get all the warranties, and of course, the contractor wants payment."

"Oh, okay," answered Maryann.

"Okay, let's get in the car and be off!" yelled out Warren. As they arrived at the airport, James was ready with the flight crew to load the luggage onto the plane. Warren told Steven to take Maryann into the aircraft because he had to go over some stuff with James. Steven nodded and gave him a thumbs-up.

"James, I'm sorry to put you in this situation. Are you sure you can handle this?" asked Warren.

James replied firmly, "Yes, sir. My men and the security staff have all been alerted and are prepared to arrest them the moment they land. And if necessary, there'd be a more brutal assault on their lives. They will get the message this location is off-limits to them."

Warren asked, "What if they don't land at the airport but get dropped off somewhere else in the community?"

"Then it will be considered a foreign invasion. All bets are off at that point," answered James. Warren noticed James's smile as he said the words *foreign invasion*. Warren understood the quiet meaning—that James, his staff, and every resident was prepared to attack these invaders with every weapon in their arsenal. He was suddenly very happy that he wasn't going to be in the residence when all this was going down.

Warren turned and saw Steven's face in the plane's window. Warren gave Steven the thumbs-up signal to make him feel better and let him know that everything was under control. The three of them quietly sat as the plane taxied to the runway, and in no time, they were in the air. Once they reached cruising altitude, the pilot asked Warren for some landing clarification.

"We are going to Bonners Ferry in Northern Idaho, and you want to take a STOL plane to land on your property, correct?" asked the pilot.

"Yes," answered Warren.

"Okay, then the best landing is in Canada, right over the border. You can pick up a STOL aircraft that can fly you directly to your property. I will radio ahead to have the plane ready to go once we land, okay?" asked the pilot.

"Great. Thank you," replied Steven and Warren; Maryann only smiled. She wasn't sure what was going on.

A little while later, Warren got up and turned to Steven and said, "One of us should learn to fly. I'm going to check out the cockpit."

As Warren closed the cockpit door behind him, Steven turned to Maryann and asked her, "What's the matter? You seem very tense and uncomfortable."

Maryann stared at him, wondering what she should say. Steven, sensing something was really wrong, moved closer to her and quietly said, "I want to help. Tell me what's upsetting you."

Maryann broke her silence with a question. "Where are we going, and why?"

"We are going to the house we call the Eagle's Nest in Northern Idaho. We got a call from the builder that the renovations we ordered are completed, and we are going to inspect them. If they are done to our satisfaction, we have to pay the builder. It is that simple."

"Who is your Uncle John, and why did he call?" asked Maryann.

"Oh, you know him as Admiral Gregory," answered Steven.

"What? Admiral Gregory is your uncle?" asked Maryann, now even more confused.

Steven took a deep breath and, looking at the floor, said, "Yes, he is our uncle, and he told us MSS put a hit out on you."

Maryann said, "Oh my God. Yes, I know. He already told me that, but I was hoping he would have solved that problem by now."

Steven said, "Don't worry. Warren and I have your back."

Maryann said, "Yeah, for how long?" Her words gave away her frustration and fear. And as the words slipped out of her mouth, she felt immediately vulnerable.

"Maryann, haven't you ever realized my brother is in love with you?" Steven studied Maryann's face for a reaction to what he just said. They both looked at each other and said nothing. Steven finally said, "I guess not."

Now Maryann looked down at the floor, and Steven said, "I've known since the day MS-13 surrounded our home. Do you remember that day?"

"Yes," said Maryann. "Warren told me to go to the safe house."

"Yes, he did, but that night, he told me that if things went wrong, I was to get you and bring you back to our house and give

176

you an envelope that would have explained everything to you. And I was to look out for you and take care of you. I read the letter in the envelope that night. It said he loves you. Warren would not have left you. Uncle John and James, the security guy for the property, told him to leave and they would handle it. Some of the renovations to the Eagle's Nest were made for you to come and live with him. He truly loves you."

Maryann began to relax a little, when Steven looked again straight into her face and asked, "Do you have any feelings for him?"

Maryann looked back and said, "I always felt comfortable with him, never afraid. But the business we were in was dangerous, and I always had my guard up, so I can't fully say yes or no."

Suddenly the cockpit door opened, and out stepped Warren. He said, "Why the long faces? We are almost to the airport, and the STOL plane is ready as soon as we land. Steven, is everything okay?"

"Yes," Steven said, smiling. "I expect all of us are just a little tired."

Warren looked at Maryann and asked, "Is everything okay?"

"Yes, but I am pretty tired. It seems like I've spent the last forty-eight hours flying on planes. I'd like to get into a comfortable bed and sleep for the next two days."

Warren looked at her and said, "I think that can be arranged," and smiled at her. Maryann stared at Warren, remembering every word that Steven had said. She felt, for the very first time, that she *could* love him. A boatload of confusing emotions came up in her mind. To silence them, she closed her eyes and fell fast asleep.

As the plane landed, Warren started to shake Maryann's shoulder. "Wake up," Warren said. "Maryann, we've arrived. Wake up… Maryann, wakeup. We've landed. We have to get onto the other plane."

"Oh, I'm sorry," Maryann said as she woke up. "I guess I was exhausted from all this flying."

"Okay, do you need help getting off?" asked Warren.

"No, I'm okay now," answered Maryann. "But how are we getting the luggage on the next plane?"

"The crew will handle that," said Warren.

As the crew was loading the luggage, Steven asked the pilot, "How long does it take to get to Bonners Ferry?"

"Fifteen to twenty minutes," said the pilot. "The tricky part is landing on your mountain. I have seen the landing strip but have never landed there. But don't worry, I've landed on other short-landing airfields, and this plane is specifically designed to do just that. Okay, buckle up. We are about to take off."

As the plane took off, the three of them grabbed one another's hands in the hope of protecting one another. Warren leaned over to Maryann and put his arm around her and told her, "Don't worry. It will be okay."

Maryann smiled back at him and said, "Thanks, that means a lot to me."

"Okay," said the pilot, "stow all equipment and get into the landing position." The three of them looked at one another in puzzlement.

"That's a joke, people," the pilot smiled, then he continued, "But I wanted to tell you we are on the landing approach. We should touch down in a couple minutes."

Suddenly, the wheels touched the ground. The plane gradually came to a stop, and the pilot turned the plane around. He proceeded up the mountain runway to a building on the side. As the aircraft came to a stop, a man walked out of the building and waved to Warren. The man told them to walk down to the main house and that he would put the luggage on the golf cart and bring it down for them.

The walk to the main house was all downhill, so it was an easy walk on the beautiful property. The views of the valley and the water were breathtaking, especially as the sun was beginning to set. When they got to the front door of the main house, the door opened, and another man said, "Warren and Steven, I presume?"

"Is that you, Chris?" Maryann asked, recognizing his voice before she saw his face.

"Yes, it is, Maryann. It's good to see you again. I hear my system worked flawlessly."

"Yes, it did. It worked perfectly. I couldn't have asked for a better outcome."

"Thank you," said Chris.

Chris continued, "I figured you would all be tired and would not want to do the walk-through immediately, so we have scheduled it for tomorrow at eleven a.m. After the walk-through, if everything is acceptable, an executive officer of Black Ops will be here for the signing of all the papers. Is that agreeable with you?"

Warren and Steve replied, "That's perfect."

"Great. I will see you tomorrow at eleven, and by the way, the refrigerator is stocked with food, as is the food pantry, so if you get hungry, there's plenty to eat."

Steven asked, "Is anyone hungry?"

"Yeah, coffee and any kind of sandwich would be just what the taste buds and my stomach ordered," said Warren.

Warren turned and asked Maryann, "Would you like something to eat?"

"Sure, I'll have a sandwich too and a cup of tea," Maryann replied.

"Okay, I will let Steven know. Please make yourself comfortable," said Warren.

As they started to eat their evening sandwiches, Warren's cell phone rang. It was James, calling from Puerto Aventuras.

"Hey, James, what's up? How is that problem getting resolved?" asked Warren.

"Not sure," James replied. His voice was grave and severe. "But I think you should come down here. I think you are going to want to see this."

Warren took the phone off speakerphone and walked out of the room.

Once he was no longer within earshot, he started talking again. "What do you mean I should come back? You told me you could handle this. Can you? Yes or no?"

"We already handled it, but the MSS are sending robots after you. I thought you and your brother might want to see one of them.

These aren't Star Wars-type robots but more like Terminator-looking robots. Up close, they look human."

"Okay, I'll fly down on the next plane, but my brother will stay here. I will let you know when I should arrive."

"Good. Looking forward to seeing you and showing you this robot soldier. Until then, bye."

After everyone went to bed, Warren called the pilot who flew them to the Eagle's Nest and told him he needed to fly back and catch a plane to Puerto Aventuras, Mexico. The pilot told Warren he would make all the reservations for him and pick him up in an hour.

CHAPTER 26

"James, hi, this is Warren. I am en route. Should touch down at the airport in Puerto Aventuras in the next ten minutes."

"Okay, I will meet you at the airport," James replied.

James picked up Warren and headed toward the airport warehouse, where the robot was being held. Once inside, James started to explain what exactly had happened. "Warren, I don't think you and your brother are safe. These robots were dropped in by parachutes directly onto your property. Two followed the road into the quicksand trap you designed. The other five were cut down by your security system. When we took off the skin of the robot, we found that all the metal parts have markings on them. We have determined that these parts were machined by US companies."

"That makes no sense," Warren stated, then he picked up his cell phone and called Uncle John.

"Admiral, this is Warren. We have a situation. I'm sending you a text picture of an MSS robot that was sent to kill us. Have you ever seen this before? The strange thing is, the metal parts have US markings on them."

"What do you mean US markings?" asked Gregory.

"The parts are marked with machine markings that show that US companies made these parts. That means they were made by US companies or stolen by China and then assembled by China or some other government."

"I see the markings," said Admiral Gregory. "These are top-secret prototypes from our robot program. I guess when China hacked the Lockheed Martin computer system, they stole this technology. I have to alert them."

"Hey, the robot's eyes are opening!" yelled one of the security guards. "It's raising his gun."

BANG! BANG! The robot fired straight toward Warren.

BANG! BANG! BANG! The security guard immediately fired back, hitting the robot directly in the head. Its eyes closed, and its metal body went limp.

James yelled, "Warren's hit. Call the medic!" The security guard called for help and then ran out of the room to get a medic.

Warren's cell was on the floor. The admiral's voice was heard yelling from it, "Warren, Warren, what is going on? What's happening there? Warren, Warren!"

"Admiral, this is James. Warren has been hit, and it doesn't look good."

The medic came running in.

"Hold on, Admiral, the medic is here," James said.

"Can you stabilize him? We need to get him out of there!" shouted the admiral.

"Yes, I need to cauterize the wound. He can travel in an hour," answered the medic.

"Admiral, did you hear that?" asked James.

"Yes," replied the admiral. "And thank you, James. I am now going to need your assistance. In forty-five minutes, there will be a supersonic jet landing at your airport. Put Warren on it then pick a spot, dig a hole, and bury any and all of Warren's stuff in it. And as far as anyone knows, Warren died there tonight and you buried him at that chosen spot. I don't want the MSS to revisit you. Make sure the funeral looks real. Do you understand?"

"Perfectly, Admiral. I'm former Special Forces, and Warren is a special guy to us. We will handle everything. But what do you want me to do with the robot?" asked James.

"Place it in a well-secured location. My people will pick it up on the way back from dropping off Warren."

"But where are you taking him?" asked James.

"EI," answered the admiral. "Goodbye, James. And thanks again." As soon as the admiral got off the phone with James, he called Steven.

"Hi, Steven, this is—"

"Yeah, hi, Uncle," said Steven, cutting him off.

"Steven, listen!" his uncle roared. "Warren's been shot! I think he's going to be okay, but I'm flying him to EI."

"EI?" asked Steven.

"Easter Island," answered his uncle. "I suggest you get there ASAP."

"Okay, can you get us a ride on a fast plane?" asked Steven.

"A plane can be at your landing field in forty-five minutes. Be ready. It has a ten-minute window before the satellites of our enemies will spot it. At nine minutes and forty-five seconds, it will vanish, so be ready and be on it."

Steven said, "Got it. We will be ready."

Just as Steven hung up his cell phone, Maryann walked into the room, still a little sleepy. "Who was that? Where is Warren?" asked Maryann.

"Warren is in Mexico," said Steven slowly.

"Well, who was it? And *where* is Warren?" Maryann asked again, wiping the sleep from her eyes.

"There's been a shooting," said Steven.

Maryann quickly put her hands to her face and said, "Please, God, no." Steven watched the tears run down her face. "Is Warren all right?" Maryann screamed.

"He's okay. He's being flown to a military hospital," said Steven.

"Can we see him? I need to see him. I need to tell him I love him," Maryann said through her tears. "I need to tell him I love him," she said again.

Steven smiled and said, "A plane will be here on the mountain in forty minutes. We need to get to the runway." They both stuffed their backpacks and then jumped into a Jeep to drive up to the runway. As they pulled up to the runway, they heard the blare of a helicopter engine. Shortly after, they saw a Navy Osprey aircraft begin to land on the runway.

Maryann said to Steven, "I never thought we would be using this runway this soon, but thank God you guys thought of this possibility." Steven just nodded his head as he entered the aircraft. As soon as the two of them sat down, the Osprey lifted off. When the aircraft reached cruising height, the pilot seemed to turn on the afterburners.

Time seemed to blur as Steven looked out the plane's window. Maryann had fallen asleep on his shoulder, and Steven thought that was probably a good thing. The copilot called out to Steven, "We are thirty minutes from EI."

As the copilot completed his announcement, Maryann lifted her head and asked, "What is EI?"

"Easter Island," replied Steven.

"Easter Island?" Maryann repeated.

"You know, the little island off the coast of Chile, about a thousand miles," said Steven.

"Why does the US military have a base on Easter Island?" asked Maryann.

"The US military doesn't. NASA does. It is for an emergency landing of the space shuttle. But they have a full hospital staffed with military doctors and marine guards, so it is a little more than just a NASA landing strip," replied Steven.

The pilot announced, "We are starting our descent. Please keep your seat belts on until we have landed. Thank you."

As the plane landed, a military man came out to meet them.

"Good morning, Maryann and Steven. I'm Dr. Lee, your brother's doctor. Come this way."

"How is Warren doing?" asked Maryann.

"He is doing much better. We told him you were coming, and he seemed very excited to see both of you."

"Were there any complications?" asked Steven.

"Yes, there were, and your brother is a fortunate man. The bullet went clear through his shoulder. He was lucky because that bullet was poison-tipped. Had it remained in his body, he would have died." Steven looked over at Maryann to make sure she was okay. Tears were streaming down her face.

Steven leaned over and said, "It's okay. He's alive." Hearing his words, Maryann put a smile on her face and started to wipe away her tears. The doctor kept talking, but as they turned the corner, Maryann heard Warren's voice, and she began to run toward it. As she turned the last corner, she finally saw Warren sitting in a chair. His entire chest was bandaged up to his neck, and his left arm was extended out by a brace.

Suddenly Dr. Lee shouted, "Don't hug him! His entire upper body is still recovering from surgery." As the two met, they couldn't figure out how to embrace, so Maryann finally found comfort in holding his right hand. The nurse quickly found a chair for Maryann and placed it right next to Warren.

Holding her hand, Warren said, "I missed you," and kissed her hand. Maryann smiled, and Warren continued, "And I never want you to be away from me." Warren looked into Maryann's eyes and said, "Will you mar—"

Maryann stopped him from finishing. "Yes, yes, of course!" she said.

Steven motioned to Dr. Lee and the nurse to move out of the room, and he said, "We'll give you two some time."

"Thank you," Maryann and Warren said at the same time, smiling, with their heads touching. When the door closed and they were finally alone, Maryann leaned closer to Warren, careful not to touch any injured parts, and they kissed.

ABOUT THE AUTHOR

Gary's love of a good story started when his uncle, an undercover agent for the CIA, spoke about his missions in Southeast Asia. His uncle witnessed life not being a straight line but one with lots of twists and turns, ups and downs, and one where only the strong-minded individuals reach their goals.

Gary went to work in the insurance and investment industry where he helped his clients by protecting them and their family from life's what ifs. He guided them through and successfully turned their goals into reality. After thirty years of growing his insurance and investment practice into a very successful business, he took a break from his work to write his first book. The inspiration for his book was the drug drop he witnessed as he jogged around a local park. His characters are defined by the twists and turns of his own life and the stories he has heard from his clients on what made them a success.

As he began to tell people about his book, their reaction convinced him he had a good story, like the ones his uncle once told.

CPSIA information can be obtained
at www.ICGtesting.com
Printed in the USA
LVHW032326220421
685284LV00005B/75